Crowned 2:

The Return of a Savage

Deshon Dreamz

Previously In Crowned

Ashura stood at the sink washing her hands as she prepared to leave her office for the day. She was tired. Lately, her thoughts had been heavily on Vince. The things that he confessed to before she killed him replayed in her thoughts all day long. He was responsible for the death of both her mother and father, and there was nothing that she could do about it.

Nothing could stop the pain in her heart from knowing that her husband was the reason that both her mother and father weren't here on earth with her. She cried, then cried some more when that reality set in. Then, she had to deal with the others that he sent. Him knowing who she was all this time and only marrying her because of the money he knew she had didn't shock her as much as knowing that he'd ordered all the attacks and had attempted to take her life. He was a coward; there was no other way to describe him.

Ashura had changed for him, and that was her first mistake. She didn't just change for him, but she wanted a different life. She wanted a regular marriage and children; she wanted all the things that she saw her parents have. Her freshman year in college had taught her a lot. Things that she would take to her grave. She didn't care what life threw at her, being the woman that she was—she would learn balance. She would learn to accept the things in her life that she could not change, and deal with those things accordingly. It wasn't necessary to bury her old self; she had to embrace it. She had to embrace the fact that her past was a big part of her future, and that there were people out there who wanted her dead.

She wouldn't lose a wink of sleep behind it.

Her eyes moved toward the door when a knock sounded at it. Wondering who it was, she left the water running so that the person couldn't hear her footsteps as she grabbed her purse and backed into the large stall. The knock sounded again, but this time with a shallow "maintenance" added to the end of it.

Ashura relaxed a little bit and was about to walk out of the stall until she heard the door open. She quickly got up on the toilet so that her feet weren't seen. She listened as he pushed stall after stall door open. Peeking over the top of the stall, she saw him holding a gun in his hand and her heart dropped.

Her eyebrows lowered as she watched him move down to the other stall and look through it.

Slowly, very carefully, Ashura wrapped her bag around her body before she climbed above the stall to cross over the top of it. Moving in silence, she didn't hear a sound outside of the sink still running. She watched him look around before he pulled a phone out of his pocket.

"She's definitely still here. I saw her walk toward the bathroom, but I don't see her now."

She listened closely as she crossed over two more stalls, waiting for him to continue speaking to whoever was on the other side of the phone.

"I think she's close. You want me to leave? I wanted to wait until I laid eyes on her. Are you sure?"

Ashura balanced herself on the toilet as she grabbed the knife out of her purse. He was in there to kill her.

She continued to squat on the toilet as she listened to him.

"Where are the others?"

She couldn't make out the voice on the other end of the phone, but she knew it was a man. Before the janitor could get out of the restroom, she jumped down off the toilet with a silent thump and crept out of the stall. Coming up behind him, she took the blade across his throat. She moved back to let him fall as she looked toward the door.

All these years, she'd fought to suppress the woman that she once was. She wanted to be different and better, and live a normal life, but she realized in this moment that she had spent the last five years of her life lying to herself. Being a woman that she didn't know, attempting to love a man who she was never completely happy with. Suppressing the beast within her. The savage. The being that didn't care about taking a life and didn't care about love. Didn't give a fuck about happiness or hope. She just wanted peace. This peace could come at the cost of anyone around her.

Nacobi was all she had. All she knew, and she was okay with that. Family had been stripped from her by the man she gave her all to. Life was snatched from her. Things she could never get back, forever unavailable. Ashura just… didn't give a fuck anymore.

She heard someone speak into the phone that the man was just holding, and decided to pick it up. "You want me dead, motherfucka?

When she didn't get a response, she grabbed the gun off the floor, checking the silencer and clip to make sure it was fully loaded. "I'm in the bathroom! Come get me, bitch! But let me motherfuckin' warn you, I'm killing everything on sight. So, send your best, or I'm coming for you! You wanted this beast, woke her up from hibernation with this bullshit, so let's fucking go!"

Disconnecting the call and throwing the phone on the ground, Ashura stepped over the body and ducked behind the wall of the bathroom as she heard a set of footsteps rushing toward her. As soon as the door to the bathroom opened, she reached around the wall. Unable to see, she released a shot that would be head level and listened to the body drop before she came around the wall.

Tiffany, her assistant, was lying on the floor with a hole straight through her throat. She had a gun in her hand and was gagging on her own blood as Ashura collected the gun from her without batting an eye.

"I knew I couldn't trust these hoes," she mumbled as she stepped over her body. "My aim is rusty, though."

She made it to the hallway, taking out two more people before she could make it to her office. Once she was there, she gathered the things that she had hidden there for a day like this. She honestly didn't think it would ever come, but here she was.

With no clue, what she was up against and how many people were there to kill her, she knew that no matter what happened, she would fight. Like she always did.

Ashura ducked behind her desk, pulling the gun that she had underneath it from its holster and looking over the small space that separated her desk from the file cabinet that sat beside it. Seeing the other janitor that Vince had hired coming through the glass door, before she could think, she stood and pointed her gun at him. A clean head shot before he knew what happened. She didn't even know who was who anymore. Anyone with a gun was getting shot.

She quickly grabbed her other bag and wrapped it around her as she made it back out of her office. Her heart was beating at a regular tempo, and she was slightly surprised by that.

She dialed a number on her phone.

"VIP."

"I need a special."

"Location?"

"Office."

"How many rooms?

"Five."

"I was already outside, Ashura.

Ashura slid the phone into her bag as she saw movement come from the opposite end of the hallway. She ducked behind a cracked door. Peeking around it to see who the person was, she noticed that they wore all black, with a mask covering their face.

She pressed her back against the wall, then took a step out and raising her gun before the person snatched their mask off, causing her heart to drop. Loyalty in this day and age clearly didn't mean shit.

"What the fuck are you doing here?!"

Zero's head snapped up and his eyes connected with Ashura's. He slowly held his hands up as he examined her. "I ain't here to hurt you, Ashura!"

"So, what the fuck are you doing here, Cole?"

Cole exhaled. Gripping the black mask in his hand as he looked at her, he said, "I'm here on orders."

"Orders from whom?" Ashura shouted. "Open your fucking mouth!"

"Your husband."

Ashura's eyes bounced all over him. "He's fucking dead. You know that, right?"

Cole nodded. "I'm not here to kill you!"

"My janitor and assistant just tried to kill me, so I don't believe shit at this point!"

"Just put the gun down."

He was stalling. She knew he was, but she couldn't bring herself to pull the trigger. "Cole, tell me what's going on."

The response she received was the feeling of cold steel pressed into the side of her head. The gun clicked as if they were disengaging the safety, and Ashura's heart dropped.

"Damn, you killed my whole team, Ashura."

That voice was… too familiar.

What the fuck did she walk in on? Why was he here?

Nacobi felt tears gather in her eyes as she pulled the gun from her back. She was torn between love and loyalty. Against her heart, she placed the gun to the back of the head of the love of her life.

The Meeting

Six Months Before…

The intensity in Cole's face reflected that of Anthony's entire demeanor.

Anthony leaned forward and pulled the picture of the woman he was supposed to take a bullet for—if need be—from the table in front of him. Her entire existence was all that mattered as of late in his life; whether it was her life or her death, he would have a hand in it. She was beautiful, that was the first thing he noticed. The very immediate second thing was the darkness in her eyes. Though they held a warm brown hue, he could tell that she had a different side to her, one that wasn't reflected in the image he held.

Cole was experiencing different emotions. "What the fuck we supposed to do with this, man? You asking us to do the impossible."

"This task is one you consider impossible? I've heard of Code Zero and the way you two operate. This is small compared to what you've done for others in the past. I just need this situation handled at a different angle. That's it."

Anthony was still admiring the image in his hands when his attention was grabbed by the last statement that came from Reeves. “They can’t know that we are there for them?”

“They won’t accept it. These women are strong, and they handle shit on their own, but I want this to be done differently.”

“What the fuck is the point?” Cole snapped as he stretched his legs in front of him. “This is not even what we do, Anthony,” Cole spoke in a tranquil tone. “We don’t protect people. This is not what we do,” he again reiterated as his irritation reached a level of complete annoyance.

Anthony continued to admire the image in front of him. For the first time in a long time, a job held more than just a payout for him. He couldn’t avoid the steeliness his heart felt at the mention of following through with their initial assignment. Was he supposed to kill her? Kill her and her partner then move the fuck on, but the proposition that was being presented to him sounded more appealing for more than one reason.

“So, you want us to avoid the initial contract that was signed with her husband, and accept your offer not only to forgo killing them, but protect them from anyone that is sent to kill them?”

“That’s exactly what I want you two to do. Trust me,” Reeves said as he clipped the end of his cigar. “You would fare better being on their good side than any other side. These women have endured a lot, and the contract you signed is married to a man who doesn’t have a fucking soul. All he wants is to have her murdered for money."

"That has nothing to do with us, Anthony," Cole spoke. "We don't need a reason; we never need a reason! We just do what needs to be done. In this instance, what needs to be done is we need to honor the initial contract." He turned his attention to Reeves. "The initial contract is to kill. That's what we do. I ain't no fucking bodyguard."

Reeves shook his head. He knew that if anyone was a threat to Ashura and Nacobi, it was these two men sitting across from him. When he found out that they were the ones assigned to the hit placed on them by Ashura's husband, he knew he had to intervene. Over the years of being their connect, he'd developed a bond with them, and he didn't want to see them killed due to the greed of Ashura's husband.

Reeves considered killing Vince a while ago. He was about to put a plan into place to have him killed, but one day, Ashura felt the need to express her love for her husband. Reeves could look at her and see that she loved him. He knew how it felt to have love snatched away, so he decided against killing him.

Vince was a fraud, though, Reeves he was. He just prayed that if ever the time came when Ashura had to handle Vince, she wouldn't allow love to interfere with what she needed to do.

"I want the two of you on this side of things; the side that doesn't place your life in more danger than it will be if you decide to void the contract that you signed with Vince and go into business with me. Regardless of the outcome of this meeting, there will be protection put in place for them that will counteract any attempts that are placed on their lives. I don't mind spending the money to keep them safe. Those two are as close to me as family gets, and if need be, I'll go broke to protect them. That won't happen before I kill everyone that poses a threat to them, but I will."

"You fucking this one?" Cole asked as he held up Nacobi's picture. "Is that why you want them safe? She fucking you too?"

Reeves clenched his teeth against his cigar before he released a dry chuckle. "First thing, watch your fucking mouth." He removed the cigar from his mouth and glared at Cole. "I look at these two as family. I know you heard me say that earlier. As beautiful as Nacobi is, I don't fuck family. I protect them."

What Reeves left off was the fact that he had indeed tried to have something more with Nacobi. She was honest in revealing her lack of attraction. As she stated, "You fine, but you old as fuck! That would be like fucking my daddy, and that shit is just gross, bruh!" After the second attempt and getting a similar response, Reeves gave up all hopes of ever having Nacobi.

Cole wondered why he was there. He knew the job they needed to do and was more than willing to get it done. Whoever Ashura

Trenton was, her husband wanted her dead, and he had peeled off a pretty penny to get that done. He glanced down at the picture, a small smirk covering his face. He could admit that the siren who was better known as Nano was a beautiful woman, but Nacobi Miles had rubbed someone the wrong way, and now, all he could see her as was a target. The most alluring and beautiful target he may ever have, but one who had to be handled in a timely manner so that they could receive the rest of their payout.

Cole placed the picture on the table, trying to push the tug he felt in his gut to the back of his mind. "Again, I ain't no bodyguard! Tried that shit! Failed at it. I would rather just get it over with."

Anthony knew that Cole didn't mean that. The woman in the picture meant too much for him to just kill her. "We'll do it."

Cole's head snapped into Anthony's direction. "What you mean we'll do it? Not the fuck we won't!"

"Draw up the contract," Anthony said, looking at Reeves.

Reeves smiled. "I'm glad you could see my side of things. I will double the offer, as stated, and I will provide you with every detail on Nacobi and Ashura." He leaned back in his seat and crossed his legs. "This means that you may need to handle Vince Combs somewhere down the line. I don't see him allowing you two to leave them alive long. The pressure to kill them will come. He is also not the only one who wants them dead. I will tell you now; this will require your undivided attention."

"We will handle that shit when it needs to be handled." Anthony stood and looked over at Cole, who was shaking his head and mumbling a few explicit words as he grabbed the brim of his fitted cap to adjust it. "Don't call my phone about shit but money," Anthony stated as both gentlemen walked out of the room.

1

Where We Left Off...

Code Zero...

Cole held his hands above his head and inhaled slowly. "Baby girl..."

"Don't say shit," Nacobi spat as she stepped into view of Ashura, who still had her gun trained on Cole as well.

When Nacobi saw, Anthony standing there with a gun to the back of her best friend's head, her heart dropped. "What the fuck is this?"

"Nacobi, put the gun down," Anthony coached.

"I ain't putting down shit." Nacobi's eyes moved back to Cole as he stood there as relaxed as he could be. He didn't seem fazed by the fact that she had a gun to his head, and that was the scariest part of this situation that they were in.

Cole knew Nacobi was more than capable of pulling the trigger and ending his life. With the life he lived, he wasn't sure he didn't deserve for her to pull the trigger. He could feel Nacobi's anger radiating off of her. She was pissed. He didn't have a way to fix it without speaking to her. He didn't want her to find out like this; he cared about her too much.

"Can you just listen to me?"

"I thought I told you not to fucking talk!"

Ashura released a chuckle that bordered on satanic. "Nano, I don't want to kill yo nigga, but the way my trigger finger set up…"

"Listen," Nano released in a low voice. "I don't know what the fuck this nigga up to, but fraud shit is something I can't handle. No matter how good the dick is!"

Cole smirked. "You just gon' talk about me as if I'm—"

"Shut up!" Nacobi straightened her arm, pressing the gun deeper into the side of Cole's head. "I can't believe this, Cole. What are you doing here? So, all this shit between us has been fake?"

"Hell nah!"

"I said shut up!"

"But you asked me a question!"

"I don't give a fuck! Don't speak!"

"Ashura."

Anthony's voice penetrated through Ashura's anger. "What?"

"Just think, love. If I wanted to kill you, I could have done that shit a long time ago." He removed the gun from her head and watched as she took her gun off Cole and placed it between his eyes. He smirked. "I like that aggressive shit, and you know that, so you can get that gun out my face."

"She better fucking not," Nano snapped.

"Same with you," Anthony stated in a calm voice as he looked at Nacobi. "If my nigga wanted you dead then you would be dead. That's not what we here for."

"Then why the fuck is you here, Anthony?" Ashura kept her gun on him, but her finger was nowhere near the trigger, whereas Nacobi had her finger on the trigger, and one slip of her finger would take Cole's life.

"I'm here to protect you, Nacobi," Cole took a risk and spoke.

"I'm here to protect *you*!" Anthony stated as he looked at Ashura. "We were sent by Reeves."

Nacobi took her eyes off Cole to look at Anthony before she returned her eyes to Cole. "What?"

"Vince hired us to kill the both of you. The initial order was sent down by him. I don't know why the fuck Cole didn't make that clear when he started talking."

"I was caught off guard," Cole admitted.

"We had every intention of going through with that job until Reeves approached us."

"What the fuck did Reeves say?" Nacobi asked, her eyes skirting from Cole to Anthony.

"He told us everything we needed to know about you two and made a counter offer. We don't usually work that way, but we made an exception. We took the contract with Reeves."

"But he did," Ashura pressed, a moue expression overtaking her face. "He sent others!"

"I was there with you to protect you, Ashura!"

"You fucking failed!"

Anthony looked at her sideways. "I've never failed you once. I never will! I know about the hit in the streets while you were on your way to meet her. I was taking out the second truck that you didn't see while you handled the one in the front. I sat outside of your house when you killed those two motherfuckas that snuck in through the side. If for one moment I thought you couldn't handle them, I would have intervened. I watched you kill Tiffany because that bitch deserved it. She was fucking your husband, and though she was a part of my team, Vince somehow got to her."

"This is some bullshit," Nacobi mumbled.

"Can you get this gun from behind my head, Nacobi? The shit is nerve wrecking," Cole added as he shifted in his stance. "You don't want to kill me!"

"You wanna bet, my nigga?" Nacobi pressed through clenched teeth. "I'll blow yo shit all over that wall like new decorations in this bitch. Don't press me."

"But he just said—"

"I don't give a fuck what he just said. I don't know him, and apparently, I don't know you very well neither."

"I've had my dick inside of you," Cole stated in a low voice, shocking everyone that stood in the small square in the center of the room. "I've had my dick in you a lot."

"Whatttttttt," Ashura whispered.

"Stop talking, Cole," Nacobi stated as she pushed him up against the wall, his back pressing against the wall as he looked down the barrel of her gun. "I was fucking you because you fine as fuck, your dick is big, and your head game is on Saturn. But clearly, I was thinking wrong because beyond all that, I thought you were honest."

Cole's eyes lowered as he watched her. "Get this gun out of my face, Nano. I've never lied to you, and I am more than honest!"

"How is that when you didn't even tell me who you were? If y'all not lying about that."

"I would never hurt you, Nacobi!"

Before Nacobi could respond, bullets came flying through the building, causing her words to get caught in her throat. She was about to start shooting back until Cole grabbed her and pulled her to the ground. Always having Ashura on her mind to protect, she looked up and saw Anthony pulling her to the ground as well.

"What the fuck!" Nacobi yelled as she scrambled on the ground.

Cole held her tight as more bullets flew through the walls of Ashura's office building.

When the shooting stopped, Cole grabbed Nacobi and lifted her off the ground as if she weighed nothing.

Anthony carried Ashura in front of him as he headed toward the closet that he knew was bulletproof. He had it built, and made sure it was just enough room for the four of them to fit in. It was equipped with every gun you could name, bulletproof vests, and artillery that was worthy of the US Army. At first, he figured it was too much for one man who just wanted his wife killed. But when he discovered that there were others who wanted Nano and Ashura killed as well, he knew it was needed. Anthony reluctantly released Ashura once he closed the door securely behind them. She moved out of his reach as soon as her feet hit the ground.

"What the fuck is going on?" Ashura yelled as she looked at Anthony.

"You got niggas after your fucking head, that's what!"

2

"What do you mean I have niggas after me?"

"Put this on," Anthony stated as he attempted to hand her a bulletproof vest.

She slapped it down and turned cold eyes to him. "I ain't putting on shit! How did you know this closet was here?" She looked around the closet before she looked back at him. "How the fuck did this closet get here?"

"Don't be stubborn right now, Ashura!"

"You need to start talking to me," Ashura said as she got in his face. "What is going on?"

"I promise to explain it to you, baby." Anthony bent down to pick up the vest and slid it over Ashura's head before he pulled her closer to him. "Do what I tell you so that I can get us the hell out of here. Then be pissed at me. Fuck me, slap me, do whatever you want. Just let me get you out of here."

Ashura decided to allow him to strap the vest around her. She wasn't stupid by a long shot. If Anthony was telling the truth and was indeed there to protect them, then she would allow him to do what he apparently was getting paid for. If for one second she thought it was something other than that, she would handle that as well.

"Fine," she mumbled as he checked the clip in a gun then handed it to her before handing her another one.

"I ain't not got damn, baby," Nano snapped at Cole as he tried to assist her with putting on her bulletproof vest.

She snatched it from him and tugged it over her head as he bit down on his teeth. His eyes bounced over her face as he tried to hold his smile back. Seeing her pissed at him surprisingly made him smile. With Nacobi, he learned it was better to have her show some emotion than none at all.

"Lying, cheating, dirty ass niggas," she mumbled as she pulled the Velcro together and tightened the vest.

"I've never lied to you, and I sure in the hell never cheated."

"How am I supposed to believe that?"

"Because I'm telling you!"

"You wouldn't be the first nigga to lie to my face, and I'm sure you won't be the last!"

"The faster you stop grouping me with the fuck boys of your past, the better off we'll be!"

"Tuh!" Nacobi smacked her lips and shook her head.

"I promise to explain everything to you, Nacobi. Just do me the honor of hearing me out."

She turned to him with a mug on her face. "Nigga, you out of favors! I just stopped myself from putting a bullet through your head. That's all my favors for a while."

She turned back around and stumbled back, making her ass brush against Cole. She felt his hands on her waist and his dick on her ass. She became even more pissed.

"What the fuck," she hissed as she turned to him.

"You mad close to my shit," Cole stated with a shrug as he tried to adjust his dick in his pants. "I'm still a man who's attracted to you whether you pissed at me or not!"

"So, you got niggas shooting at you, and your dick is hard? Really?"

"You trippin' on me because you had your ass against me and my dick is hard? Have you seen yourself lately, Nacobi?" Cole leaned in closer to her. "Do you know how fat that ass is? My dick will forever be hard! I don't give a fuck about niggas shooting. I'll die with a hard dick fucking with yo ass."

"Nigga, whatever!"

Cole smirked as he reached for Nacobi, who surprisingly didn't fight him when he had her in his arms. "Fuck me, slap me, do whatever you want! Just let me get you out of here," Cole mocked Anthony.

"Fuck you, nigga." Anthony chuckled as he fixed Ashura's vest.

Ashura and Nacobi shared a look that read 'how the hell are they so calm when people are shooting at us?' "This isn't your first time being shot at, is it Anthony?"

"Far from either of our first time." Anthony looked into Ashura's eyes. "I promise to tell you everything, sweetheart. Just follow me. Stay behind me, keep your head down, and keep a full clip. Don't check out on me."

Ashura moistened her lips and nodded her head. She had a million and one walls up. The only person in this closet that she trusted more than she trusted herself was Nacobi. She knew she had her back through whatever, and she was prepared to go to war with anyone if Nano was by her side during that battle.

Cole's face became stern when he heard voices. He slowly moved Nacobi behind him as he grabbed two guns off the shelf and turned to her. She was livid with him, and he couldn't blame her, but he needed her to listen and follow him for him to have any chance of making things right.

“Listen, I know you pissed at me,” Cole spoke in a low voice. “But trust me when I tell you that the only reason I am in your life is to keep you protected. Now that I know you, I want to do a lot more than that, but I want you to follow me so that I can get you out of here.”

He checked the gun before he placed it in her hand and grabbed another for himself. “Will you trust me to get us out of here?”

Nacobi checked the clip of the gun, then the safety before she looked back at Cole, giving him a sly smirk. “Fuck you and suck my dick!”

Both Ashura and Anthony laughed at the blank expression on Cole’s face.

Nacobi placed one gun in her back and clutched the other one in her hand. “I’ll follow you, Cole. Just don’t think shit is going to be good when we get out of here.”

“I don’t expect that,” Cole stated as he stepped around her to get in her face. “I hear all that shit, Nacobi. I hear what you telling me, but I'm telling you I ain't through with you. Far from done.”

Nacobi went to open her mouth before Cole opened his mouth again. “I ain't about to go back and forth witcho ass right now, Nacobi. You gon’ fucking listen until I can get us out of here.”

Ashura looked on, waiting for Nacobi to come back with something fly to say like she always did.

"Yeah," Nacobi mumbled as she examined the seriousness in Cole's eyes.

"Thank you!"

Nacobi eyed him. "Where is your vest?"

"I can't fit them."

"Then what the fuck are you using for protection?"

"I don't need it. As long as you have one, that's all that matters. Just let me get us out of here, love."

Nacobi inhaled and nodded her head.

Ashura looked at Nacobi with a smirk on her face.

"Don't talk to me, bitch," Nacobi snapped at her.

Ashura raised her hands up and chuckled. "You got it, Sis."

Nacobi shot her eyes to Ashura before she flipped her off with the hand that held the gun. She hated the word "sis." She thought most times when another woman called her sis, it was fake love being shown. What she and Ashura had was far from fake, so the word "sis" had no room in their friendship.

"We will move north of the building, and y'all move south," Anthony stated, directing his words to Cole.

"Hold the fuck up!" Ashura looked at Anthony. "Who is we? I'm not leaving her!"

"Ashura," Anthony groaned.

"I don't care, Anthony. I'm not taking my eyes off Nano."

"We don't have time for this shit, Ashura."

"It's fine, Ashura," Nacobi assured her. "If this nigga on some slick shit, I won't think twice about shooting him."

Cole liked that. He wouldn't expect her to handle herself any other way.

"I got her, Ashura," Cole stated, addressing Ashura for the first time.

She squinted as she walked over to him. "You don't know me, Cole. I don't have shit else in this life but her. You don't understand how much she means to me, and if something happens to her, I'll kill everything you love. From pets to grandparents."

Ashura smiled as Cole frowned. He didn't take well to threats, but he understood how she felt. He didn't have many things left that he cherished, but the woman in front of him literally had no one but Nacobi. "I promise you, I'll protect her."

Ashura felt secure in the fact that her message had been relayed. "Cool, let's get out of here."

Crowned 2: The Return of a Savage

"Shu- Shu," Nacobi called out to Ashura.

"I got you for whatever, Nano!"

"You swear?"

"I promise."

3

Anthony led Ashura through the north side of her office building, knowing the ins and outs of it like the back of his hand.

Ashura wasn't too far behind him, holding her gun in her hand tightly as she listened closely to the voices that seemed to be getting in proximity to them.

"Stay close," Anthony whispered over his shoulder as they rounded the corner.

Three men stood on the opposite end of the hall, clearly gathering detail. Ashura watched Anthony as he drew his gun and killed two while she moved from behind him to take out the last one.

Anthony stood straight and looked at Ashura as she shrugged. "What?"

"I asked you to stay behind me."

"I was behind you. I came from behind you to help. Now I'm going back behind you."

Anthony shook his head as he grabbed her by her waist and pushed her behind him before they both began to move down the hall.

"Shoot anything that moves, Ashura."

"You really don't have to tell me twice," Ashura mumbled as they slowly advanced down the hallway slowly. Her eyes trained to pick up any movement.

She knew Nacobi and Cole were on the other side of the building, so she wasn't concerned about running into them. She just wanted to get out of this building alive so that she could get somewhere and clear her head. She for damn sure at this point wasn't going back to Anthony's.

Anthony gripped Ashura as he came to a stop, hearing voices coming from the end of the hall. "Behind me."

Ashura nodded her head as if she was going to listen, when in reality, she had her own agenda. Sub-plotting on how she could get away from both the people here to kill her and Anthony. Keeping her body close to the wall, she watched Anthony move up and take two men out before they were even aware of his presence.

Bullets came flying through the wall toward them. Backtracking, Anthony grabbed Ashura and turned to go back in the direction they came. Ashura covered his back, dropping body after body as they came around the corner after them. Her heart was beating at a steady rate, and her mind was more settled than it had been in a while. She was content. Even after killing people.

Once Anthony saw that they were in the clear, he placed Ashura on her feet and looked down at her.

"What?"

"I can see now that you a little extra. But you shooting niggas and shit got me ready to do something to you. Nasty shit."

"Anthony, you won't ever get to touch me again."

Anthony laughed as if she had just told the funniest joke. "Bullshit! You can believe that if you want, but that's far from the truth. The fact of the matter is, you belong to me know. I gave you that disclaimer before I ever put this dick in yo life, so that shit is real, Ashura. Get with it."

"I ain't getting with a damn thing. You said that to me when I thought you were honest, but now that I know you not, that shit ain't gon' fly."

"I don't have time for this shit right now! You want to argue, do that when we get to safety. Right now, I need you to follow me and do as I ask of you. Cool?"

Ashura rolled her eyes. "Yeah… whatever."

Eventually, after killing what seemed like ten men, they made it to the parking garage, where they would stay and wait in Cole and

Nano. So that they weren't caught slipping, Anthony parked his bulletproof Escalade at the door he knew Cole would come out of.

Ashura sat in the front seat, fuming. She was pissed off for a number of reasons.

"I never once lied to you."

Ashura sucked her teeth and crossed her arms. "No, actually that's all you did. You lied to me about who you were. What you were. You let me cry on your shoulder about Vince, when in reality, you were the one sent to finish the job that others couldn't." Ashura wasn't doing a good job of shielding the hurt she felt. She didn't want to be vulnerable anymore. She was tired of that, and more than anything, she didn't want to be weak for or around Anthony. She refused.

"Reeves will tell you once we get out of this shit. Was I sent to kill you initially? Yes, I was. On the verge of fulfilling the contract that I signed with Vince. Before I knew you or him for that matter.

"Did you know that he was beating my ass?"

"No, I didn't know that shit. I don't work for cowards."

"Any man who has to hire another man to kill his wife is in my eyes a coward. Any man that signs on for that shit is a coward too."

Anthony leaned his head back in the headrest of the driver seat. That hit home for him. In the years that he and Cole had been doing hits, they'd never hit a woman. Would never take a job to kill any women or children. That was against the code that they set; they went against everything to gain this contract because of the number that was thrown at them. It would've have been their biggest payout. Big enough to retire them. That was always the goal, make enough money to get out and never have to return to this lifestyle, but things never worked out that way. They hadn't gotten a job big enough yet, but taking out Ashura and Nacobi would have done it for them. Looking back at it, Anthony knew both their opinions were tainted when they decided to pick this job up. This should have never been an assignment to begin with. But then, he wouldn't know who the hell Ashura Trenton was. That thought bothered him.

"Look, Ashura, you right. I've never killed a woman or a child, and I should not have gone into contract with Vince's bitch ass. The numbers he threw at me had my head fucked up, that's all that was. It isn't something that I'm proud of, and I'm glad Reeves reached out, and we didn't try to finish that contract."

Ashura would be lying if she said she didn't understand. Anthony was working in a very dangerous field, a field where almost anything could happen. You couldn't be an assassin and have a heart at the same time. You had to be cold. Had to be distant. Blank almost.

"Oh, I wasn't worried. Others have been sent, and you and Cole would've ended up just like them. Those numbers Vince was throwing at you was on my dime. Nigga put out a hit on me with my own got damn money. Imagine that bullshit."

"Ashura, I didn't know any of that. I just got a job presented to me with a lot of money on the price tag. I'm sorry if you don't believe me. I don't have a reason to lie to you. I don't get anything from that shit. Reeves countered the offer, and I took the offer and ended up being your protection versus your enemy."

Ashura's leg shook as she looked out the window on her side of the car. "How long have you been doing this?"

"Three years."

"How many people have you killed?"

"Not counting the ones in there," he stated, tilting his head toward the building. "Thirty hits."

"You've killed thirty people? People you don't even know?"

"It was part of the job that I signed up for, so yes, I did."

"That's some wack shit."

"It was the job."

"Yeah, I know, and I get it."

"Do you really? Because from here, it just looks like you judging me."

"How can I judge you? I've done things that I regret. Things that I'm not proud of. I've hurt innocent people, and that's something that I'll eventually have to deal with and answer to, and the same goes for you. Anthony, you and I, we are no different."

"That's where you're wrong. Us two. Me and you. We way different."

"How?"

"We just are. I killed people because of a contract. An agreement. I didn't need any more of a reason to take people's lives, and I should have. You only kill to survive. I do that shit in my sleep, with no worry or concern for anyone else. I only care about me and making money. So much so that I killed people like that shit didn't matter to me. Life! My life or anyone else's life didn't matter to me, but I'm done with that shit now, Ashura."

"And why are you all of a sudden done, Anthony?"

"It's not all of a sudden!"

"So, why the fuck are you done, Anthony? We can skip the technicalities."

Anthony glanced over at Ashura with his jaw set in a stern expression. "I'm done with this lifestyle and the things that come along with it. I want something different now."

What Anthony wouldn't say is that he wanted something more with Ashura, but he didn't plan to rush her. He considered her past and the pain that she had endured at the hands of her ex-husband, so he didn't want to pressure her to accept what he had planned for his future, a future she would be heavily involved in.

"I'm glad you want better for yourself, Anthony. You're still young, and you have plenty of time to still enjoy your youth.

"I ain't that fucking young, Ashura. I actually did enjoy my youth outside of all this extra shit I was into. I'm a grown ass man, though. If anyone should know that, it should be you."

Ashura exhaled and rolled her eyes. She didn't need any more convincing; she knew Anthony was a grown man in every sense of the word. He even had his life together more than men far older than him.

"When are we leaving? The faster I'm away from you, the better off I'll be.

Anthony chuckled as he relaxed in his seat. "We waiting."

4

"You gon' get us killed."

Cole grabbed the bridge of his nose before he turned back to Nacobi.

"Baby—"

"Don't call me that, nigga!"

Cole inhaled as he looked Nacobi in her eyes. "Nacobi, please just trust me for one minute. I need you to follow me! You just said that you would less than fifteen minutes ago!"

"Sike, I lied, nigga," she threw over her shoulder as she walked in front of him, her gun held tight in her hand, her steps featherlike as she rounded the corner.

Whoever was after them wanted them dead. There was no doubt about that.

"I don't understand why you're so pissed, Nacobi. You are doing the fucking most right now!"

"Nah, I just don't like liars."

Cole grabbed Nacobi and pulled her back to him, leading her into a small office space and closing the door. She was about to go off until the look in his eyes stilled her.

"What do you want, Nacobi?"

"I don't want shit from you?" She just mugged Cole as he stood in front of her. Close. So, close that her mind didn't register that he was touching her until it was too late to fight him off.

"I apologized! I tried to explain why I kept this shit from you! What else do you want from me?"

Nacobi shook her head as he walked her back into the wall. "You so full of shit!"

"I care about you!"

"Bullshit," Nacobi snapped in his face. He towered over her, his hand planted on each side of her head as he looked down at her. His glare empty while his scent radiated off of him, causing her thoughts to swim. "You don't care about anyone but yourself."

Cole groaned as he took a step back, scratching his head with the end of the gun before he exhaled. "That shit so far from the truth, ma. I care about you! I'll fuck someone up behind you! You sexy, beautiful to me, Nacobi. You're funny and outgoing. You are the exact opposite of me, but I adore everything about you. Plus, yo pussy curves to my dick, which means you were made for me. You are for me. Fuck all the extra shit. I don't need you to be boss chick

Nano right now. I need you to be the Nano I deal with behind closed doors. The one who listens to me. The one who moans my name when I got my dick inside of her. That's the motherfucka I need right now! Try riding for someone other than Ashura! I'm here! I'm your man! I make you cum and put money in yo mothafuckin pocket! Ride for Cole!"

"You want me to trust you," Nacobi hissed. "You sat in my face and lied to me, Cole! How am I supposed to trust you? Let alone ride for when ain't shit about you loyal!"

"I never lied to you, Nacobi. Everything that I said to you was the truth. I care about you, that's the only reason I'm still doing this shit."

Nacobi inhaled before shaking her hair out of her face. "I don't want to keep going back and forth with you, especially not right now. Can we get out of here?"

Cole shook his head. "That's what I been trying to do, but you wanna argue and shit," he mumbled as he turned to walk in front of Nacobi and out of the office that they stood in. He knew he would have a lot of work to do to earn her trust, but he was willing to do whatever.

Stepping out of the office first, Cole looked both ways before pulling Nacobi close behind him and releasing a sigh of relief when she didn't withdraw from him. He went to the left, moving toward the parking garage where he knew Anthony and Ashura were waiting. His mission at this point was to get Nacobi to the car with no harm done to her.

He turned the corner of the long hallway and pulled Nacobi behind him. “Stay close to me.”

When Nacobi didn’t verbally respond to him, he looked back to make sure she was okay. When he saw that she was fine, outside of the pissed off expression on her face, he turned around to move further down the hall when a bullet flew into his chest.

“Cole!”

Stumbling back, Cole was able to get a few shots off before he collapsed to the ground. He saw the person that shot him drop as he slid down the wall, feeling his head getting light.

“Shit,” he hissed as he focused on breathing.

Nacobi moved around Cole, letting her gun go off wildly down the hall, hitting anything that came around the corner. She didn’t stop until she didn’t see anyone else coming.

Nacobi grabbed Cole and propped him up against the wall. Thinking fast, she took off her top shirt and balled it in her hands to apply pressure on Cole’s wound. She couldn’t look in his eyes. She didn’t want to know if he was breathing or not. She couldn’t think about him leaving her. Terror, emotions, most apparently fear, raced through her, tears falling freely from her eyes.

"Fuck, Cole!" she cried as she pressed down on his chest. So much blood, too much. "I told you that you needed a vest!"

Cole grimaced as she pressed down on his chest. "I'm too big for them shits. Besides, there were only three of them. I had to make sure you had one."

Nacobi held her head down as more tears gathered in her eyes and her hands began to shake. "You have to get to a hospital!"

"I just need to get to my spot," Cole groaned as he attempted to stand, only to slide back down the wall in his haste.

"Stop moving, Cole, please! Let me call Anthony! Where is your phone?"

Cole reached into his jeans and pulled out a phone.

Nacobi kept pressing on his chest while looking at the phone. It wasn't his regular phone, and that didn't sit well with her. "Whose phone is that?"

Cole clenched his teeth and looked up at Nacobi. "What?"

"I asked whose phone that is? It's not yours."

"It is mine."

"I ain't never seen it!"

Cole shook his head. "Seriously? You wanna do this right now?"

Nacobi shook her head and bit her lip. “Such a fucking liar!”

Cole grabbed his chest when she pressed too hard on his wound. “It’s a one-way line, Nacobi. I can only call Code.”

“And who the fuck is Code?”

“Anthony,” Cole groaned. “How many times I gotta tell you, I’m not a liar. I’m a lot of things, Nano, but I’m not a liar, and I don’t want to hurt you.”

Nacobi eased up off of his chest, applying the pressure that was needed as he dialed Anthony.

“Yo…”

“I’m hit. Last hallway near the garage.”

“Here we come.”

Cole dropped the phone from his ear and looked up at Nacobi through lowered eyes. She wouldn’t look at him, but he wasn’t expecting the reaction she had to him getting shot. Since meeting her and getting to know her, he’d determined that she wasn’t an emotional person. The only emotion she expressed freely in front of him was anger. But this Nacobi had fear in her eyes; it wasn’t fear of the people who were shooting at them, it was a fear of losing him. It was at this moment that he knew that no matter how much she fought it, she felt something deep for him, and he would never allow her to walk away from him. Not without a fight.

"This shit hurts like a motherfucka," Cole groaned as his eyes got low.

"Just stay woke, Cole. Don't close your eyes!"

Anthony and Ashura came around the corner with guns out. As they approached them, Ashura ran straight to Nacobi.

"You alright?"

Nacobi nodded her head before she glanced at Cole. "He needs to get to the hospital!"

"We can't take him to the hospital," Anthony declined. "We need to get him to his spot."

Nacobi became pissed. "What the fuck is at his spot that's so special? We need to get him to a hospital. He's bleeding out!"

Cole was focusing on breathing, on staying alive. His eyes didn't leave Nacobi's face.

"Let's just get him in the truck."

"And to the hospital," Nacobi tacked on, letting it be known that their only destination would be the hospital.

5

Nacobi was scared. Terrified. That didn't happen often, but when it did, it was a very surreal experience.

"I don't know how to feel," Nacobi mumbled to Ashura. "This man has been lying to me for months, but somehow, deep down inside, I still care. I still…"

"Love him," Ashura provided.

Nacobi's entire body tensed. "I don't love him."

Ashura ran her fingers through Nacobi's hair. They were sitting in the waiting room at the hospital, impatiently waiting for an update on Cole. Nacobi was still struggling with the emotions running through her. She'd faced death before, had guns put to her head, had people threaten her life, but she had never been as scared as she was the moment Cole got shot. Her heart still hadn't returned to its normal rate. She didn't know if it was love she felt for Cole, she just knew whatever it was, it was strong and demanding. It needed her attention, it needed to be addressed, and it had no plans of going away.

"Have you called Reeves?"

Ashura shook her head. "I haven't yet, but I plan to. He should have told us about all of this, if we would've have known, I could have handled Vince's ass a long time ago before he could hire more people to come after us."

Nacobi nodded her head as it rested in Ashura's lap.

Ashura's strokes in Nacobi's' hair slowed as she looked down at her. "You need clean clothes, boo. You need to get this blood off you."

Closing her eyes, Nacobi released a shuddering breath before she nodded again. "I don't want to leave him."

"We'll wait for Anthony to come back."

Nacobi almost fell out of Ashura's lap when Anthony and the doctor came around the corner. "How is he? Is he okay? Can I see him?" she asked the doctor in a rush, everything forming into one long sentence.

Anthony and the doctor shared a glance before they both smirked. The doctor was extremely attractive, and far too young to know what the hell he was doing. He looked as if he was in his early twenties. Both Nacobi and Ashura were gawking at him. Although the moment was serious, they couldn't help but take him in. All his chocolate sexiness.

"Well, damn," Ashura mumbled.

"Girllll, that's what my ass was saying," Nacobi replied absently.

The doctor smiled. "You must be Nano," the handsome doctor asked as he extended his hand to her.

Nacobi looked down at her hands and frowned. "I don't want to touch anyone or anything with his blood all over me."

"That's understandable," the doctor stated as he withdrew his hand. "Mr. Remington lost a lot of blood. We had to do emergency surgery to remove the bullet. He will make a full recovery after a small healing period. He lost more blood during the surgery to remove the bullet, but he should be just fine. He woke up asking for *his Nano*. He is resting now, but you can go back and see him."

Nacobi blushed as her heart seemed to skip a beat. She was glad to hear that he was okay, and even happier about the fact that he wasn't blaming her for him getting shot. She knew it was her fault; she was her natural self, stubborn and difficult. If she would have been listening or even answered him when he called her, he would not have lost focus. They wouldn't be here right now.

Nacobi released a deep sigh as Ashura came up beside her, eyeing Anthony and the doctor, who seemed to be very familiar with each other. It didn't take much for her to figure out that they knew each other.

Anthony looked down at Ashura. "He will be here for the next five days. After that, he'll go home, where he will need a nurse."

Nacobi's ears perked up at that. "A nurse? For what?"

"To assist him in his recovery," the doctor answered. "He will need a lot of attention, though I have a feeling that a man like Cole won't be down for long at all. He still needs some help."

Nacobi nodded her head before she glanced over at Ashura then to Anthony. Nervously, her eyes finally landed on the doctor. "Is that something that I can do?"

Ashura looked at Nacobi like she had two heads. Anthony's expression reflected confusion as well, while the doctor just smiled at Nacobi.

"It would be small stuff, like changing his bandages, cleaning his wound, helping him around, helping him bathe. Small things like that."

Nacobi nodded. "I can do that. He won't need a nurse."

"Whattttt," Ashura let out.

"Shut up," Nacobi snapped. "Damn."

"Let me find out, though," Ashura teased.

"I just…" Nacobi looked around; all three of them were looking at her with unconvinced expressions. "I want to make sure he's okay. He took a bullet because of me, so I think it's only right that I look out for him."

"Girl, look out for yo man. No one is saying you shouldn't," Ashura added with resolve.

Nacobi closed her eyes and inhaled before she turned diabolic eyes on Ashura. "You get on my nerves so bad, bitch."

"Oh well," Ashura tossed at her before she childishly stuck out her tongue.

Nacobi looked over at the doctor. "Can I see him?"

He nodded before he took a step back. "Right this way."

"Tell him I said to stay up Kane," Ashura tossed at Nacobi's back, earning her a middle finger. "Don't die! Keep hope alive or whatever and what not!"

She laughed and shook her head before her gaze landed on Anthony. Her smile and laugh evaporated as they did so. "Who was he?"

Anthony crossed his arms over his chest. "Who was who?"

"The doctor. I know this isn't your first time meeting him. You were far too comfortable, and if I've learned anything about you, I know that you don't get comfortable fast."

Anthony stepped closer to her. "I don't know him."

"Don't lie to me."

Anthony dropped his arms and huffed. "Why the fuck are you so difficult?"

"There isn't anything difficult about what I asked you, though. Just say you don't want to tell me, Anthony."

"It's not that I don't want to tell you."

"Is that why we came to this hospital in particular? Couldn't we go to Regional since it was closer?

"Let me get you home. We can talk about that when we get there. I don't want to discuss that here."

"I'm not leaving until Nacobi leaves. I think you already knew that."

"Nacobi's leaving tonight too," Anthony snapped.

Drawing back, Ashura grimaced at him. "What do you mean she's leaving tonight? Didn't you just hear her say that she was staying with Cole?"

Anthony looked around the hospital before looking back down at her. Grabbing her arm gently, tugging her toward privacy so that their conversation couldn't be heard.

Once they were far enough from the general population, he spoke. "Cole is leaving tonight too, Ashura."

"What?"

"He's checking out, and we will set him up at his apartment. He will heal faster that way."

"What in the whole hell?" Ashura groaned as she scratched her head. "You make him sound like a robot. He needs the same amount of time to heal as anyone else."

Anthony stepped closer to her. "No, actually he doesn't."

"So, what you are telling me is, somehow Cole heals faster than the normal human being?"

"I'm not saying all that," Anthony stated with aggression. "Can we just get out of here? I promise to answer any questions that you have. Right now, Nacobi and Cole are being transported to his place."

Ashura grabbed her phone out of her pocket and dialed Nacobi, all the while not taking her eyes off Anthony, who was rolling his eyes in his head.

"Hello," Nacobi answered.

"Where are you?"

Nacobi inhaled at the other end of the phone. "I'm in Cole's room, but I don't think I will be here long. He keeps saying something about transport. I'm lost as fuck. Like, how is this nigga even talking right now, and he just got shot?"

Ashura looked up at Anthony as he stared down at her. “It’s some weird shit going on.”

“Can you just come with me, Ashura?” Anthony pleaded with his hands in a prayer position. “We are going to the same place as Cole and Nacobi.”

After eyeing him for a moment, she released her resolve in a deep sigh. “Fine, come on. Nacobi, I’m on my way to you.”

“Okay.”

Sliding her phone back into the pocket of her jeans, Ashura followed Anthony out of the hospital.

6

He watched her through hooded eyes as she walked around his loft, fighting the smile that tugged at his lips. She seemed nervous, which was something new for him to witness. It was refreshing, though.

"Nacobi," he groaned in a dry voice.

Her head snapped in his direction as she stopped moving. "Are you okay, do you need something?"

Cole smiled as he moved up in the bed.

Nacobi threw her hands up, gauze and alcohol flying out of the tray she was holding. "Like how the fuck are you moving? Like, you almost died. I saw it with my own eyes. You were about to black out; you had blood coming from everywhere, it seemed. I still have your blood on me, Cole."

"Calm down, love."

"Fuccckkkk that," Nacobi exclaimed as she walked over to him. "Why didn't you die?"

Cole frowned before he smiled. “Would you rather that I died, Nacobi?”

“What I would like to know is why you didn’t!”

Cole’s somber look only added to Nacobi’s frustration. “I appreciate you for being here, Nacobi.”

“Tell me, Cole.”

“It’s a long ass story. Longggg and annoying.”

When Nacobi glared at him like she wanted to take his head off, Cole knew that he had pushed the subject a little too far.

“Since I was young as hell, I’ve always been into technology, always wanting to know how things work and what makes things, blow, tick, defuse, combust. All that. My mother put me in technology schools from middle to high school, then, of course, college. I was in all types of groups and shit, organizations, and clubs. My senior year in college, I met this older guy who was running this test on folk. It was a serum they were testing for the military, some under the table shit. I was young, didn’t know what I was really getting into, but I signed up for the serum. It was one shot, makes you heal fast as fuck. Once I got it, I said—”

“Wait… what?” Nacobi’s hand extended out to the side of her in confusion. “What the hell are you talking about?”

"I took a serum in college that makes me heal fast. As long as I can get to either the serum or stop the bleeding in a timely manner, then I won't die."

Nacobi scrunched up her face in a way that would have made Cole laugh out loud if the situation wasn't so serious.

"You got life and bullshit fucked up!" Nacobi stated with a dry laugh before she shook her head, waving her hand in the air dismissively. "You trying to tell me that you some alien or some shit?"

Cole dropped his head. "I'm not an alien. I was born and raised in Dallas. But just like you, in college, I got into some things that changed my life. There are a lot of things that I want to talk to you about, things I want to tell you about me, Nacobi. Things I don't share with other people. I want you to know everything about me."

"Wait… you serious?"

"I am."

"So, basically, you can't die?"

"Basically."

Nacobi was in deep thought.

"So, I just saw you almost die! I don't know why you aren't dead! You took a bullet to the chest! I saw the shit with my own eyes. Hell, I covered your wound so that you wouldn't bleed out! Now I don't even see a hole in you!"

Cole's dark eyes turned to Nacobi's. "You saved my life!"

"Fuck all that, nigga! Are you Logan?"

"Who the hell is Logan?"

"Wolverine from X-Men!"

Cole's frowned. "I'm not..."

Waving her hand dismissively with a mug on her face, Nacobi stood, "I'm from the hood, and I've seen a lot of shit, but I don't have time to be fucking Barnacle Boy!"

"That's not even..."

"Are. YOU. A. Science Project?"

"What?!"

"But was you in the ocean for decades like Captain America but you still fine as fuck because you were froze, and shit?"

Cole hung his head as a smile caressed his face. "I'll tell you everything. Just don't freak out on me, okay?"

“So, can you die?”

“I can’t die from anything but old age, or an ailment that kills me so fast that the serum can’t cure me. I can die, though Nacobi, it's just a matter of time and the situation. I want to make sure that's clear. Headshots, old age, natural causes…"

"Like cancer?"

Cole nodded his head. "I can't die from something that I can heal from. But if it's terminal, outside of the regular treatments for something, such as cancer, there is nothing that the serum can do to save me."

Nacobi's eyes rounded as she looked at Cole. "Wait, do you have cancer?"

Cole shook his head. "No, I don't, Nacobi."

Nacobi shook her head as she sat down in a chair close to the door of Cole's room. For the first time since entering the apartment, she was able to look around. The last time she was there, they were making love as if it was the last time they would ever see each other. A sense of peace washed over her when her eyes landed on Cole. Even after the news he just delivered, she was happy he was okay. Guilt. Something that she wasn't used to dealing with had overtaken her thinking process. Now that she knew that he wouldn't die, she felt like her head was clearer. She was still confused as hell by the news, he had just delivered.

"I would like to show you something," Cole spoke in a soft voice in the tenebrous room.

Nacobi looked up at him, trying to make out his face. “What would…”

Her question was interrupted by Ashura and Anthony walking into the room. Sliding the dimmer on the wall up, Anthony brought some light into the room.

His eyes landed on Cole before they moved to Nacobi. He could tell by the look on Nacobi’s face that Cole had let her in on *them*.

Nacobi stood and turned to Anthony. “Did you get the shot too?”

“Yes, he did,” Ashura supplied as she walked around Anthony. She stood in front of Nacobi, silently sending a signal that she was about to do something crazy. Before Nacobi could open her mouth, Ashura produced a gun out of nowhere and placed it to Anthony’s head.

Her eyes brimmed with unshed tears as she looked at him, letting Anthony know that she was not only pissed, but hurt. But why?

“Does that shit work against headshots, Anthony?” Ashura spoke, her voice low and level. Monotone to the point it caused apprehensiveness on Anthony’s part.

“Ashura,” he spoke cautiously.

"Answer me," she screamed, pressing the gun further into Anthony's head.

Nacobi and Cole were both stuck in their positions, not sure what to do or what happened that quick to make Ashura snap.

"No, I die from a headshot like anyone else would."

"Then don't stop us, Anthony. Don't try to stop us from leaving."

Cole cautiously spoke, "Y'all can't leave. Not right now."

"But we are," Ashura snapped as Nacobi remained quiet. "Let's go, Nano!"

Not questioning Ashura, Nacobi moved to follow her.

"Ashura, listen."

Ashura straightened her arm. "We're leaving, and there isn't anything you can say to stop us. I'll be in contact with you."

Making one final attempt at stopping them, Cole called out to Nacobi, but she didn't answer as they left his apartment.

7

Her head was spinning. Hadn't stopped since yesterday, and didn't show any signs of stopping.

"No contact with them until I talk to Reeves and find out what the hell is going on, Nacobi. I'm serious."

Nacobi scrunched up her face. "Okay, damn! You are acting like I don't understand English. No contact with Cole, I get it."

"I'm just saying," Ashura threw out with a chuckle. "I know how you are, and I don't want you to contact him. No matter how horny you get."

Nacobi threw a side eye at Ashura. "Girl, fuck you!"

Ashura threw her head back and laughed. Knowing Nacobi, she was possibly on the verge of breaking and calling Cole to get her right, even though it had only been a few days since they'd seen them.

They were camped out at Nacobi's, and though Cole had never been inside her house, he'd been outside of it too many times to count. It wasn't the best hiding place, but it was better than going back to Ashura's.

Ashura sat with her foot propped on the edge of the couch while her chin rested on her knees. She exhaled deeply, causing the fly aways from her messy bun to swoosh out of her face, somehow reflecting her mood. Lost. Caught off guard. Confused.

Ashura wasn't sure who to trust. Her head was still messed up from the confession that Anthony gave her back at her office building, then the second confession that he made in the car on the way to Cole's. She didn't understand how she didn't see it; how she didn't know that he was there with ill intent. To know that on top of everything else, they still had people after them, she couldn't help but feel horrible. She felt like she was dragging Nacobi down with her, and she never intended to do that. She loved her too much to ever to put her in any real danger.

Ashura knew that Nacobi didn't blame her for the situation that they were in, but she couldn't help but feel like she was failing, though she fought so hard to win. Her head and heart both were unsettled. How did she miss who Anthony was? He was attractive, young and—nearly indestructible.

"It was his sex game," Nacobi mumbled absently, clouded by her thoughts as well. "He snuck my ass." She released a nervous giggle before she took a long sip of her drink. She swallowed her sorrows before she sucked her teeth, sliding her tongue across the top row before clicking her jaw. "As soon as I feel like I found someone that I like… he shows his ass. How many times am I going to set myself up like that before I give up on this love shit?"

"Don't blame love."

Nacobi cocked her head to the side to glare at Ashura. "Bitch your husband has been trying to kill you for two years, he's been abusing you, he's been lying and cheating. And on top of that, the young, sexy ass brother who has been effortlessly blowing your back out, was in real life sent to kill you. Love isn't shit."

Defense Mechanisms. Most times with Nacobi, this was how she dealt with things. She didn't like the head space that negative energy put her in, so she avoided it. Dodged it and refused to confront anything that would put her in the position to address bad vibes. Bad space and clogged energy were the only things that threw her off, and she didn't need that.

"Love is not the thing that makes wanting someone complicated. It's the person that you choose to love not having the mind to love you back."

Nacobi studied her friend as she spoke. Her thoughts lingered on her statement, prompting her to ask a question that had been on her mind for a while now.

"Why did you stay with Vince, Ashura?"

Ashura glanced over at Nacobi for a moment before she broke eye contact. She sniffled before releasing a preempted chuckle. “Can we just say that I was stupid and leave it at that?”

“Well, we could, but we both know that’s not the case, so I’m going to say no. What happened?”

Ashura closed her eyes as unwanted thoughts of Vince surfaced. She didn’t want to think about him. Didn’t care to. It was a part of her life that she wanted to put behind her as soon as possible, and that wasn’t going to be something that she could do if she talked about it or continued to run from it like she was doing now.

“Vince was everything to me at one point.” She cleared her throat and tucked her leg under her before she continued to speak. “I was happy with him, Nacobi. When we first met, I was so happy. I was in love with him; he could have anything. Any part of me that he wanted, I gave him that freely, with no reservations.

I just gave, gave, gave, and gave, until I didn’t have anything else that he wanted. We were happy until the beginning of last year when his business started to struggle. After his first few deals went bad, he just changed. My business was thriving, his was suffering, and he just couldn’t handle it. His black wife being more successful than him. After a few months of me being acknowledged for my hard work, he just snapped. The first time he ever hit me was after my first award ceremony. It was just one punch, dead to my face. He said he did it because I was flirting and disrespecting him at the event, but that wasn't it."

She stopped to look over at Nacobi, who was listening intently with a mug on her face.

"He did it because he was jealous for a completely different reason. He wanted the success that I gained. I did everything to help that fucking coward, and he was spitting on me! Beating my ass and apologizing so sincerely that I thought he meant it. Until the next time, I was covering a black eye with concealer."

Nacobi's jaw clenched in anger. "I swear, if his ass wasn't dead, I'd kill him myself. But, you didn't answer my question. Why did you stay?"

Ashura eyed Nacobi before she smiled slightly. "I stayed for love. I stayed because I was stupid behind his no-good ass, and I believed him every single time he said that he would never hurt me again. I stayed because I was in denial about how bad my situation with him was. I stayed for stability. Not that I couldn't take care of myself, no, I could do that with no issues. I stayed because he looked good for me. For normalcy, for consistency. I stayed for hope. For lies and bullshit. I stayed for Vince. I just… stayed."

Nacobi shook her head. "I'm sorry for what he did to you, Ashura. I'm sorry about your parents, and I'm sorry that I wasn't there for you. I feel like shit for that. Not knowing what you were going through, not taking the time to pay attention. I was so caught up in Romeo's bullshit, I just dropped the ball. I failed you, and I'm sorry."

Ashura shook her head as she reached out to grab Nacobi's hand. "I told you I hid it from you, Nano. I hid it from everyone. I was going through my own personal hell, and I didn't have time to deal with anything else. If anyone has failed in this friendship, it's my ass. It's me. I'm sorry, and I promise to never hide anything else from you ever again."

Nacobi leaned over and wrapped her arms around Ashura before she placed a sloppy kiss on her cheek. Ashura groaned her disgust and attempted to push Nacobi off of her, but she wouldn't budge.

"Ewwww, get off!"

Nacobi released her with a smile on her face. "I love you, bitch!"

Ashura rolled her eyes and wiped her cheek. "So aggy."

8

Cole was sloppy drunk. Drunk to the point that he hadn't moved out of his bed once in the last twenty-four hours. This was another rarity for Cole. He had stopped getting drunk a long time ago during his college days, after a series of unfortunate events. The only exception to this situation was that he was in the house.

"This shit too much," he grumbled as he moved to grab his ringing phone. "What, Danielle?" he snapped in an indignant manner as he leaned his head back on his pillow, setting his bottle down and running his hand down his face.

"Is that how you answer the phone for the mother of your child?"

"That shit is to be determined, so let's not even speak that into the atmosphere."

Danielle chuckled on the other end of the phone, glancing over at her son as he played with toys on the floor. She rolled her eyes before she returned her attention to the phone. Being a mother wasn't something that she wanted to do. She'd always wanted to be single, able to do whatever she wanted, whenever she wanted. She was over the initial shock of being a mother, sometimes, though, she wished she didn't have kids.

"I remember telling you not to call me anymore."

"Cole, you know I can't do that. I thought you wanted to do a test."

Cole rolled over on his back and looked up at the ceiling. This thing with Danielle was dragging him, on top of what he was dealing with where Nacobi was concerned. Three days and no communication with her was slowly killing him. He missed her scent, touch, and taste. So, he wanted to be numb. At least for a moment, but Danielle seemed to pop back up at the wrong time, coincidentally.

"I'll call you when I'm ready to do the test, Danielle. I don't want you calling—"

"Wow, Cole. I never took you as the deadbeat type."

"What are you talking about?" Cole slurred. "You pop back up after all these fucking years, telling me about a kid that I knew nothing about, and you expect me to just spring into Daddy mode? I don't even believe that he's mine, Danielle. I fucked you once, and I used protection."

"Yeah, you fucked me while I was with your best friend. I bet Anthony still doesn't know just how fucking shady you are."

Cole made a solid attempt at remaining calm before he exploded. “Danielle…”

“But you so loyal. Tuh! The nerve!”

“I messed up,” Cole snapped as his anger boiled over, “that’s something that I will have to handle with Anthony, but you wasn’t shit but a toss, Danielle. You know that. I hit once, and I used protection, so I don’t even need this test to let me know that your son isn’t mine. I’ll send you the court date! Until then, don’t fucking call me!”

“I need your help with something, Cole!”

Cole groaned as he held the phone. “What?”

“My fiancé… he’s missing, and I need you to help me find him. His name is Vince Combs. I think something happened to him. I think it was his shady ass wife that had something to do with him disappearing. I want you to find him or find her and get some answers for me

Cole frowned as he listened to her, trying to keep the shock of hearing that she was engaged to Vince even while he was married to Ashura out of his voice. “How the hell am I supposed to help you with that? You know that’s not my line of work.”

“I know that you are the best at tracking people, so if he’s still out there, you’d be the one that could find him.”

Cole disconnected the call and slammed his phone down on the nightstand beside him. He closed his eyes, feeling like the weight of the world was on his shoulders. *Vince was fucking Danielle? While he was married to Ashura?* So, not only was he abusing her, he was cheating on her as well. He couldn't help but to wonder just how much of this Ashura knew about. This was too much bullshit coming down at once. Too much.

"This dude was hella foul!" He hated feeling like this, and the only thing he knew for sure would pull him out of his mind state wasn't answering his calls.

The next morning, Cole woke with a headache and a hard dick. After his conversation with Danielle, he knew he needed to talk to Anthony sooner than later.

Cole pulled himself out of bed with a grunt as he went to take a hot shower. In the recesses of his mind, thoughts of his life played on a loop. His childhood was typical, two parents that loved him, normalcy, consistency. Nothing was off about the way he was raised. Yet, he always felt that he was different. Going through school, he didn't make an attempt to click with anyone. Anthony was the only friend he ever had, and he had betrayed him in an ultimate way, with a female who wasn't even worth the hassle at all.

After breakfast and calling Nacobi an estimate of twenty times to no answer, Cole finally called Anthony over so that they could have the dreaded discussion about what happened between him and Danielle.

Once Cole was dressed in his signature all-black attire, he retired to his living room with a cool drink, trying to clear his head before Anthony's arrival. When he heard Anthony at the door, he released air from his lungs as Anthony strolled in with a mug on his face. He knew that mug was a result of not speaking to Ashura.

Cole chuckled as Anthony flopped down on his couch, tossing his key on his end table and exhaling so deeply that it rumbled in his chest. They had keys to each other's places, in the case of an emergency. Like getting into something that required either of them the use of the serum, they always made sure they kept it close.

"What's up, boy," Cole asked Anthony and received a grunt in response.

Anthony ran his hand down his waves and licked his lips. "Mannn, Ashura ass on that bullshit, bruh! I don't understand her ass. All I'm trying to do is protect her, give her everything her husband couldn't give her, and she doesn't appreciate what I'm trying to be for her. Then, all her shit is in the guest room. Her scent is all over my house."

"You be sleeping in the guest room to feel closer to her and shit?" Cole joked and shook his head, knowing Anthony wasn't down that bad. When Anthony just looked at him from the corner of his eyes, Cole knew he was on to something. "Wait..."

"I did that shit one night, bruh!"

Cole laughed so hard that his head started to hurt. "I knew it! Boy, you so lame! You wanted to be covered in her scent or something?"

Anthony flipped Cole off as he slumped further down in his seat. "Why you think they trippin' on us so hard? We told them our intentions. We made that shit clear as hell."

"I mean, we didn't lie to them, but we did keep some very important things about ourselves away from them, so I can kind of understand why they were pissed off. But, Nacobi's ass can feel however she wants. She gon' have to come up off of that because I won't let her do whatever she calls herself doing for much longer. I need to see her stubborn ass. I miss her."

Anthony smiled at Cole. It was rare for him to show this much emotion behind a woman. It was rare for him to show any emotion behind anything in reality. "I know where you are coming from. I don't even know how Ashura ass got in my system so quick. She just different in all the best ways. She's quiet when she needs to be, talks and expresses herself when needed. She just got a lot of hurt left over from being with that wack ass white boy, and she's waiting for me to mess up. I'm already losing in her eyes. When I met her, when she allowed me to touch her the first time, I was losing."

Cole nodded the entire time that Anthony spoke, agreeing with everything he said. Knowing the ins and outs of the battle that he was facing with Ashura because he was in that same exact battle with Nacobi. Unrestricted pain given to you by someone that you once loved or gave your all to was something that took time and attention to get over. Cole had asked Nacobi up front to be honest with him about her feelings and stance on her ex; always wanted to be sure he wasn't fighting a losing battle with her. She was quick to assure him that he wouldn't be placed in a position to pay for someone else's mess ups. He didn't feel like he was, he felt like Nacobi was confused on what she wanted, due to his actions or lack thereof toward her or where she was concerned. He didn't want this to be dragged out. Wanted it fixed as soon as possible. He wanted everything fixed, in the open. He could deal with shit easier that way.

"I got some shit I need to run by you, Anthony."

Anthony was tired and only half listening to Cole. Stalking was exhausting as hell. "What it is?"

"You remember Danielle?"

Anthony twisted up his face. "You mean my overdramatic, thot ass ex-girlfriend, or smash buddy, or whatever the fuck?"

"Yeah her…"

"I remember shawty. Why, what's up?"

"I fucked her." Cole was never the type to beat around the bush, not even in situations like this one. "I fucked while y'all were together."

"What the fuck!" Anthony exclaimed and stood to his feet, causing Cole to do the same thing. They were in each other's face.

"Shit just happened, bruh," Cole explained. "I got drunk one night, and she came on to me. I didn't turn her down. Shit was foul—"

"Foul as fuck, Cole," Anthony spat. "Nigga, you smashed my girl? We don't do that type of shit to each other unless it's a real-life toss. I mean, Danielle was a toss, but I was in a relationship with her. You were smashing her behind my back while I was with her? Foul ass motherfucka!"

"I hit once," Cole insisted. "Just once, and I fucked up doing that. I'm sorry, bro. I was foul, I did some foul shit, and now it's coming back to bite me in my ass."

"Fuck is you talking about?"

"She was fucking Vince."

"WHAT?"

Cole shook his head. "She popped her ass back up with a three-year-old talking about some *he mine*."

"Wait…"

“I asked her for a paternity test.”

“Hold the fuck up!” Anthony made a T with his hands as he shook his head. “So, you fucked Danielle once while we were in college. She somewhere down the line met Vince and was fucking him. Now she telling you that she has a three-year-old by you?”

“Basically.”

“When were you planning to tell me this shit? When did we start keeping shit from each other, Zero?”

Cole dropped his head. “Man, this shit been dragging me. I didn’t want to keep it from you. Me fucking her was a mistake, and I know you pissed, but I didn’t intentionally smash her behind your back. I wouldn't do any shit like that to you. I wouldn’t, and you know that. I just got drunk as hell, and it just happened. I never even laid eyes on her after that night. I don’t even half way remember the shit.”

“But it did happen, and now she telling you that you have a kid? What the hell you gon’ do?”

“I hit once. I highly doubt she is telling the truth. Hell, it could be your kid as well as it could be mine. “

“Bullshit,” Anthony spat. “I strapped up every single time I ran up in her ass.”

“I strapped up too!”

"How would you remember when you were drunk?"

"Because I don't give a fuck how drunk I was, I never hit anyone raw."

"That you know of."

"Period," Cole insisted.

"How did you know Vince was fucking her?"

"She just told me that shit on the phone earlier. She said some shit about her fiancé being missing, told me his name was Vince Combs."

Anthony sat down, which prompted Cole to do so as well. Cole felt bad for more reasons than one. His loyalty was to Anthony, and he had betrayed that loyalty by being involved with Danielle. He hoped that this was something that they could recover from quickly. Anthony and Cole rarely ever got into it, but Cole knew he had crossed the line at this point.

"I don't even care about that bitch, Cole. You know that's not why I'm pissed. You my boy, bruh! I'm supposed to be able to trust you with my life."

"You mothafuckin' can," Cole insisted. "I'd jump in front of a bullet for you, my nigga. You know that shit. I regret what I did, and I would never do anything like that again. That's why I don't get drunk; I do stupid shit when I do. I'm sorry about this, Anthony, man. I made a huge mistake."

"I'm not pressed, Cole. I forgive you. Just don't hide shit from me. This is a conversation that we should have had the day after it went down. You wouldn't have said shit about it if she hadn't popped back up."

Cole knew that what Anthony said was true. He planned to take that dreadful ass night to his grave until Danielle's sudden reappearance. "Like I said, I'm sorry about it, and it won't happen again."

Anthony grabbed air in his lungs before he released it. "Bet. I know it won't though, because I no longer entertain thots. But what you gon' do if the baby is yours?"

"It's not. She won't let me see him, and I think she is just pulling this shit to get me to help her, or to keep me close for whatever reason. I don't know."

"Well, Ashura said that Vince is dead."

"Yeah, but where the fuck is the body?"

9

Cole: *Please?! Please...just call me!"*

Nacobi smiled and shook her head before replying.

Nacobi: *Why can't you call me, Cole?!*

Cole: *You got my number blocked!!!!!!!*

Nacobi laughed out loud at his overuse of the exclamation marks.

Nacobi: *Oh.*

Cole: *Come on, please? Please Nacobi. I miss you so fucking much!*

Nacobi exhaled as she sulked, dropping down on her bed in her bedroom. She missed him too, so much. But she didn't know for sure if she could trust him to love her securely. After dealing with the hurt of Romeo, she didn't want to deal with another man who was into playing games. She wanted loyalty, respect, and multiple orgasms. Cole had delivered all on all fronts until recently.

Nacobi: *I need time and space from you and this entire situation, Cole. After all, I have my life to worry about.*

Cole: *I would never allow anyone to harm you, Nacobi!*

Cole: *I don't care about anything more than I care about you!*

He was texting her far faster than she could respond.

Cole: *I'm on my way over there!*

"And he driving on top of that," Nacobi uttered with a deep sigh. "This man."

Nacobi: *You don't even know where I stay!*

Cole: *Yes, I do! I've been to your house a million times!*

"This man is crazy!"

Cole: *I'm about to come over there if you don't call me in five minutes! I'm already close!"*

“Shit,” Nacobi hissed before she exhaled. She unblocked Cole’s number and called him. The call barely connected before he answered.

“Hello!”

Why was he yelling? “Why are you yelling?”

Cole relaxed in his seat at the sound of her voice. “Damn, if I knew that was what it was going to take, then I would have said that a week ago!”

“What is it, Cole?”

“I can’t sleep, baby!”

“Cole, I don’t have time for this.”

“I can’t think, baby!”

Nacobi frowned. “Wait…”

“I can’t go on, baby!”

“Cole, are you…”

“Without you in my life!”

Nacobi rolled her eyes in her head. “Not R. Kelly, though, Cole. I mean, really?”

Cole sucked his teeth and bit his lip. “I ain’t know what else to say!”

"Cole, get up off my line, dude."

"I miss you," he breathed into the phone. "I want to see you. Make sure you good."

"I'm good."

"I need to lay eyes on you to determine that."

"I know you've laid eyes on me, Cole. I know you aren't that far."

Cole grunted as he turned down the street to Nacobi's house. She was right; he was never too far from her. Since the moment she ran into him, he's had this attraction to her. His pull to her was not as immediate as Anthony's pull to Ashura, but it was equally as strong. He wanted to protect her, not because they were getting paid. In reality, they'd stop taking payments from Reeves a while ago. Now, he wanted to protect her solely because she was his. She belonged to him in every manner, and he didn't have an issue with letting her or anyone else know that.

"You right. I'm never too far from you, Nacobi."

"So, what exactly was the point in you needing me to call you, Cole?"

"Like I said, I needed to see you. I wanna touch you, hold you in my arms, and make sure you still love me."

Nacobi closed her eyes as she placed the last dish in the dishwasher. "I care about you, Cole. Never told you that I love you. I don't want you walking around here with false hope. "I care about you deeply, but I don't love. I tried that shit and it flopped, so let's just not complicate things further by tossing that word around."

"I love you, Nacobi. I don't care that we haven't been talking long. I don't care that I'm not your favorite person right now. I love you. I want to be with you. That's all of it."

Nacobi was stuck. This conversation seemed to go in the wrong direction and fast. Love. Love?! "Love?"

Cole smiled as he pulled his car in front of her house and put it in park, readjusting the phone between his ear and his shoulder. "Yes," he spoke with pride as he climbed out of the car. "I love you, in love with you, and all that shit. So, how we finna do this? You coming out, or do I need to come inside?"

"You're confused, Cole."

"No, I'm not. My mind is clear, and my heart is yours, and I don't want that shit back."

"This is crazy," Nacobi mumbled as she rubbed the frustration out of her forehead.

"I'm 'bout to come in."

Nacobi ran to the window of her living room. Looking out, her eyes rounded in shock before she released the curtain that she had drawn back and exhaled. “Are you crazy, Cole? Ashura is here! Her ass is on a rampage, and clearly told me not to have contact with you.”

Cole smiled as he walked up the driveway, feeling like he was getting closer and closer to his prize. “I need to see you.”

Nacobi nervously paced her living room. “Shit!”

Cole looked up at the modern style home before looking at the front door. “You gon’ open the door for me?”

“Cole, I can’t.”

“Listen,” Cole stated, his tone holding a warning that Nacobi failed to take heed to. “I have a key. I don’t mind using it to come inside, though I would much rather be invited.”

“Why and how do you have a key to my house?”

“I got one made,” Cole answered with a shrug. “That is not what we are talking about right now, though, Nacobi. You gon’ open the door?”

Nacobi placed her face in her hands before she sucked her teeth. “Come back later. Cole, I just think we need time away from each other, and space. Just until Ashura and I figure out what the hell is going on. It’s too much right now. Then you throwing words around that you don’t mean. We… just need space. Just a small break.”

Cole chuckled on the other end of the line. “Bet.”

When Cole first laid eyes on Nacobi, he was invested. Now that he has deeper feelings for her... he's different.

"Cole?! What the hell are you doing?!"

Cole strolled into Nacobi's home, stroking his beard as he grabbed the middle of his jeans to pull them up. He smiled as he took in the decor of her home. It smelled like her. He missed the scent. "I came to help you pack your bags and shit."

Nacobi's face reflected her confusion. "Pack my bags for what??"

"Oh," Cole spoke with a laugh. "You said we needed space from each other. I thought we was going somewhere or some shit."

"But, you didn't think that, Cole. You know what I meant!"

"You said space."

"I also said break! As in you and I no longer together!"

Cole smiled, which was a rarity. "See, we on the same page!"

"Okay, so why are you here?!"

Cole's smile dropped as he turned to walk further into her house. "I'm gon' help you pack yo bags since you trippin' and shit." He flopped down on the couch and adjusted his fitted on his head before he licked his lips. "Where the fuck is we going, Nacobi? Break up?! Space?! The fuck?! You belong to Cole Remington! Fuck is you talmbout?!"

"You can't force me to be with you!"

"And who the fuck else you gon' be with?! I'll kill any man that touches you, and your pussy curves to my dick!"

Nacobi's jaw dropped.

"Get with the shit, baby girl! You practically married. Tell niggas you are Mrs. Remington! Yo nigga crazy as fuck, and locked with a Draco! Now, come sit on daddy lap! How was your day?"

"Really," Nacobi whispered harshly. "I… we can't do this right now, Cole."

"I love you."

Nacobi covered her ears and shook her head. "Would you stop saying that? Stop saying that!"

"Why would I stop when it's just how I feel?"

Cole took a minute to look Nacobi over. The evidence of how much he missed her radiating off of him and relaying itself in the increase of his heartbeat and the sweat forming in his palms. She looked refreshed, smooth as always. Such a natural beauty, so gracious in her natural being. Just slightly hood and outspoken. Yes, he was in love with her. Deeply in love with her."

"I can't leave right now. Not until you talk to me and tell me what's been going on with you."

Nacobi could hear Ashura walking around upstairs, and every time she moved, she got more and more nervous. Was she scared? No, but her loyalty was to Ashura, and she knew that she was serious about not having contact with Code Zero until they had all the answers. They were far from having the answers they needed. Nacobi groaned as she grabbed a smiling Cole by the arm and dragged him into her study. She closed the door once they were inside, locked it, and turned to Cole.

"What would you like to know?"

Cole looked around, taking a seat on the couch as he looked back up at Jacobi. "I said to sit in daddy's lap, Nacobi."

Jacobi shook her head, "I am not doing that!"

Cole licked his lips before his grin deepened. "Come on, baby. I know you miss me, Nacobi. You can play hard for your home girl, but I saw the look in your eyes when I got hit. I know you love me."

Nacobi became pissed with herself for even giving him the ammo to make such a statement. She was terrified when he got shot. The thought of losing him made her panic on a level that shook her to the core. She didn't know what she was feeling for Cole, but it was deep. Disturbing.

"Cole, this situation is different for me. I won't lie and say that I don't care about you. I do. But you lied to me."

"Come here, Nano. Come sit down and talk to me."

"I don't want to..."

"I didn't ask you anything, love. Come."

Reluctantly, Nacobi walked over to Cole and sat in his lap. Immediately, Cole wrapped his arms around her, inhaling her scent, and engulfing himself in her as much as he could.

"I want us to be happy, Nacobi. I want us to be together, and I don't want to hold anything from you. I want to tell you everything about me, the good and the bad. I want to be open to you. I want you to be my woman, and I don't want to share you with anyone. I want us to grow together, and I don't care what you say, I love you. I'm in love with you, and I plan to show you that every day."

Nacobi looked down at Cole, his dark eyes shadowing everything he'd just stated. He was nervous. The fear of rejection anchoring him under the weight of Nacobi. He didn't want to hear her deny him. Didn't think he could survive the blow.

"The situation with Romeo..."

"Your ex."

"Yes, he ran me through the wringer. Doing and saying shit to me that doesn't make me trust easily."

"I asked you in the beginning…"

"Cole, I was honest with you. I don't hold what he did against you, but that doesn't mean that I don't still deal with it."

"But I'm not him," Cole snapped. "I promise to keep you safe, never let harm come to you, make love to you whenever you want, whenever you need. I won't cheat on you; I won't do any of the things that he did. I promise, Nacobi."

Nacobi swallowed hard as she made an attempt to move out of Cole's lap. "This is too much, Cole. Too fast."

Cole grabbed her, stopping her movements. "Please don't shut down on me. Don't withdraw from me. Please?!"

"I'm not withdrawing from you, Cole."

"I can feel it, Nacobi. Don't."

Nacobi relaxed as her mind settled. She didn't have a choice but to acknowledge that Cole had her. She was hooked, and there was nothing she could do to help herself get away from him. She was done trying.

"Okay, Cole, but I have rules. Things we need to put into place so that we can avoid all the bullshit."

Cole smiled before biting his bottom lip. "What rules do you have?"

"Of course, my first rule is No Bitches! I mean, that's a no brainer, right? We don't need to go over that!"

Cole chuckled. "No, sweetheart, we don't need to go over that."

"I want my time when I ask for it. I like clingy. Be all over me all the time, or I'll think someone else has your attention."

"I won't have a problem doing that shit."

"Never lie to me."

"I won't."

"I want to know everything about you. The good, the bad, the ugly, and I will give you all of me in return."

Cole froze at that, which made Nacobi turn around and look at him.

"Cole?"

"I don't mind telling you everything," he spoke, his voice low, almost radiating defeat as he spoke. "I just don't want you holding the things that I've done against me. I want you to be open when I tell you things. When I show you things. When I open up to you, the shit is deep, Nacobi. It can get scary, and I don't want you to run away."

Looking at him intensely, Nacobi pondered his words. She didn't think he could tell her anything that would run her away from him. "I want you to be honest with me. Be vulnerable and open, because that's what I am."

Cole reached around her to grip the back of her neck. Gently bringing her down, he placed a soft kiss on her lips before he looked into her eyes.

"I will be."

10

Anthony: *Please call me, Ashura. You said that you would!*

Ashura stared at the text message on her phone before she looked up at Nacobi, nervously gnawing on her bottom lip. "I don't even know what to say to this man."

Nacobi leaned back in the chair, stretching her body out and propping her feet up on the pillows on the end of the couch before she adjusted the laptop in her lap. She glanced at Ashura then returned her eyes to her screen. She felt bad for Anthony, but she knew how stubborn Ashura could be when she got in one of her moods.

"I accepted a call from Cole," Nacobi mumbled under her voice, trying to not really let Ashura hear her, but of course, she did.

"You what?!"

Nacobi sat up quickly, placing her laptop on the couch beside her. "He was all whiny and stuff, and I just couldn't deny his fine ass. I just talked to him once. It was just once."

"You just talked to him once, and that's it, Nacobi?"

Nacobi peeked up at Ashura as a blush spread across her face. "Okay, sooooo…"

"Nacobi," Ashura snapped as she glared at her best friend. "Are you serious?"

Nacobi groaned as she closed her eyes.

"I asked you."

"I knowwwwww…"

"You said that you wouldn't!"

"I knowww!"

"What happened?"

Nacobi shrugged. "Nothing happened, really. He just wanted to check on me and make sure I was okay. Even after I told him a million times over the phone that I was good, he still came, and he basically just professed his love for the kid and left."

Ashura smiled as she got out of her seat. "Professed his love for you? Whatever do you mean?"

Blushing, Nacobi looked over at Ashura with worried eyes. "I think getting shot made his ass delusional. Like, something changed with him. I don't know if it's a phase or what, but I'm terrified." Releasing a frustrated groan, Nacobi allowed her shoulders to drop, showcasing her doubt. "I feel like this is moving too fast with us. I was good when it was just sex, but now it's like, I have to be open and shit. I don't like it. Why can't he just be okay with us bangin' out?"

Ashura held her laugh in. "Bangin' out?"

"Yea," Nacobi added, oblivious to the effect her words were having on Ashura. "Girl, we went to the mall a few weeks ago, and I literally had to drag a bitch because she walked up on us on some rah-rah shit."

"Wait, what happened?"

"Girlllllll," Nacobi expressed. "So, boom, I was all in PINK looking at jumpers and shit, kicking it with Cole, and some female walked up and was like 'Oh, you just gon' fuck me and leave me hanging' or something like that. I don't know. The shit rubbed me the wrong way, so I asked Cole in front of her what the fuck she meant. He hit me with some, we'll discuss it later. I was about to go off on his ass, but ol' girl said something to me and made me flip out."

"In the mall?" Ashura asked.

"Bitch, I was scrapping, hitting everything moving."

"In the mall, though? With Cole?"

Nacobi nodded her head, almost ashamed of her actions now that she looked back on them. Almost. "So, I tagged her ass. Well, I was until her friends tried to jump, but Cole wasn't having that shit. He started throwing bitches left and right."

Ashura laughed so hard that her stomach started to hurt. "Wait?! Cole?! Cool, calm, and collected Cole started throwing females?"

"Girl, that nigga turned into The Incredible Hulk so quick." Nacobi smiled as Ashura continued to crack up. "I think it was that day when he was throwing bitches like Frisbees that he became bae."

"So, what's the issue? Why can't you admit that you love him, because I know that you do, Nano? Whether or not you want to admit it, I know you do."

"Girl, that love shit is too stressful for me. You see what I went through last time. It's too complicated."

"Love is not the thing that makes wanting someone complicated. It's the person that you choose to love not having the mind to love you back."

"So, is that why you haven't called Anthony?"

Ashura blew her cheeks out as she stood. "I know that I will need to speak to him sooner than later. I'm handling my shit; you just be sure to handle yours."

***

Anthony stepped up on the porch with a frown covering his handsome face. Cole stood not too far behind him, anxious as ever. He knew his friend was pissed, but he was just glad he would be able to see Nacobi.

"She got me fucked up, bruh," Anthony murmured as he slid the key into the lock and marched into the house like he owned the place.

Nacobi, who was sitting in the living room eating fruit, immediately jumped out of her seat and reached for the gun that sat beside her. When she saw, who was at the door, she immediately relaxed.

"Where yo girl at?" Anthony asked her.

"Uhhhh…"

"Don't do that shit, Nacobi. I know she here."

Nacobi glanced at Cole, who was smiling at her as if he'd won the lotto, before she looked back at Anthony. Exhaling, she gave in rather quickly. "She's upstairs in the study. I would advise you to knock first. She has a Desert Eagle in her lap."

Anthony wasn't scared of Ashura. In fact, he was already halfway up the stairs when Nacobi finished her spiel.

Ashura laid on the couch in the study being serenaded by *Ella Mae's 10,000hours*. The words to that song spoke to her mind, heart, and body.

Why you always take so long to call me?
Know I gotta wake up in the mornin'
You know every second adds up to a minute
Need 10,000 hours
We can be so in love
Don't stop; I'm counting them up
Run the clock; I be counting them up
We can be so in love
You know every second adds up to a minute
Need 10,000 hours
We can be so in love

She groaned as she rolled over and placed her head under the cover before she flipped back over. Glancing up at her phone, which rested on the desk across from her, she contemplated calling Anthony. She was woman enough to admit that she did indeed miss him. A whole hell of a lot. But her stubbornness where he was concerned would not allow her to call him or return any of the calls or messages that he left. Still, she was having a hard time dealing with being away from him.

Ashura looked at the door when she heard her name called. She couldn't make out the voice, but she knew it wasn't Nacobi. She was about to start thinking she was delusional until she heard someone yell out.

"Aye!" His voice was so deep, penetrating. "Which room is it? I can't find her light, bright ass."

Ashura nervously scrambled off the couch, falling and hitting her knee hard on the ground before she sprang up. "Shit," she groaned as she limped over to look at herself in the small mirror that sat on Nacobi's desk in her office.

"Why am I checking myself in the mirror?" she snapped in frustration as she ran her fingers through her wild hair. She fixed her clothes before moistening her lips.

"To the right," Ashura heard Nacobi yell from the stairway, moments before the door to the study was pushed open, and Anthony walked in.

As soon as his eyes landed on her, his anger seemed to vanish; well dwindle slightly before he stepped into the room and closed the door. For what seemed like forever, they just stared at each other, looking deeply into each other's eyes as both of their hearts raced at a dangerous pace.

"What are you doing here?"

Anthony leaned against the closed door for a moment before he pushed off of it, then walked into the room and took a seat on the couch that Ashura had previously occupied.

"I came here to talk some sense into you."

Pointing at her chest, Ashura turned to him, "Talk some sense into me, huh?"

Anthony gave her an affirmative nod as he leaned back to admire her. She looked so good, rested, and relaxed. He watched her as she began to pace, a nervous gesture she would take up when she didn't know what to say or do. She snatched the hair band off her wrist and pulled her hair up into a high bun on the top of her head before she turned to glare at him.

"Ohh please, Mr. Code, enlighten me. What are you doing here? I asked you for space."

"Yeah you did, and I gave you that shit. Even after I wanted to choke you the fuck out for putting another gun to my head."

"I did what I had to do."

"I wouldn't advise you to do that shit again."

"Ain't you just gon' heal from it anyway, Wolverine?"

Anthony smiled at her. "You got jokes and shit."

"Can you please leave?" she tossed over her shoulder, slowing her steps just enough to do so."

He watched Ashura pace back and forth. The dress she wore seemingly restricting the thickness of her thighs and ass. He had to will his manhood to not ruin the moment. Ashura wasn't in the mood for extra right now, and that… what his dick had in mind for her, would for damn sure be considered extra.

"Calm down, Ashura."

Ashura stopped pacing to look at him, her eyes squinting in suspicion as she tilted her head to the side to get a good look. "I don't even know why I'm taking a chance to trust you after all this shit! How am I supposed to know if I'm dealing with *Code* bitch ass versus Anthony?"

"Code bitch ass." Anthony chuckled as he adjusted his tie. "Code and Anthony are one in the same. Code has been the one protecting you. Anthony has been the one making you cum. Shit… sometimes I let Code in to handle that shit too."

"Are you serious?"

"Dead ass."

"Are you bipolar?"

"Nope!"

"Why are you here?"

Anthony leaned forward. "We had some shit come up, and I need you to listen to what I have to say before you start flipping out."

“What is it?”

“You would know if you accepted my calls.”

“What the fuck is it?”

“Reeves wants you to leave town for a week or so, lay low until he gets things settled.”

“And why the hell hasn’t Reeves called me or accepted my calls?”

“There is no need for him to speak to you. I’m your man, I handle shit.”

Ashura wanted to slap the smirk off his handsome face, but she had other things to deal with. “So, what’s the master plan to deal with this?”

“We need both you and Nano in close proximity. We also need y'all to be off the grid for a while. So, Cole and I are taking the two of you to Fiji.”

He said it as if it was across the hall from the office they were in. Ashura twisted up her face at him. “Come again?”

“We are taking you two to Fiji for two weeks, on us.”

“You mean on Reeves.”

Anthony reared back as if he had been slapped. “The fuck? I’m not allowing another man to finance a trip for my lady and I!”

“How many times do I have to tell you that I’m not your lady, Anthony? I can’t be with a man that I don’t trust!”

“How many times do I have to tell you that you can trust me? I know shit started off rocky, and I understand the need to be guarded, but my entire purpose at this point is to keep you safe. That means going to Fiji, on me! It will be a two-week trip, so pack heavy, and leave that fucking attitude in the states. I don’t want to deal with that.”

Anthony stood from his seat and walked over to Ashura as he fixed his sports coat. Ashura watched him bring his hand up to capture her chin and tilt her head back. He moistened his lips before leaning down to kiss her a few times, pecking her lips, then looking at them intensely before kissing her again.

“Please stop thinking I’m here to hurt you. I would never do that. You should know that by now, but since you don’t, it’s my job as your man to show you that I will only touch you in ways of love, and nothing else. I ain’t that last man, never will be. Know that!”

Ashura released a tense breath when Anthony stepped back to walk out of the room. “Don’t bring no pajamas, I’ll keep you warm so that you won’t need them,” he threw over his shoulder as he left out of the office.

11

She didn’t listen to him. Didn’t take heed to what he said because she didn’t have any plans to go anywhere with Anthony.

Ashura and Nacobi were forced to leave the house to get groceries; they had no plans to be out long. Just a store run to stock up on food and hygiene products that they needed. Then back to their hideout until they got more answers.

Ashura was walking down an aisle in the produce area, pressing her fingers into an orange to test its tenderness before she tossed it around in her hand a few times. She grabbed a produce bag and tested a few more oranges before tossing them in her bag. Nacobi was across the store in the snack aisle grabbing everything that they didn’t need.

Once Ashura had everything that she wanted, she made her way to find Nacobi, who she discovered still standing in the snack aisle with her basket full of unnecessary items.

“Really, Nano?”

Nacobi looked at Ashura and smiled. “Yes, bitch! I need junk food! I can't get any dick; Aunt Flo done carried her bitch ass to my dwelling without permission, with her rude ass, and I need something to get me through. I need all this."

"You really don't, though."

"But I do…"

"Whatever." Ashura giggled as she waved her off. "Are you ready to go?"

"You got some food to cook, right? Because that was the whole purpose of this trip."

"Yes, I did, with no help from you. Thanks a lot!"

"No problem, boo." Nacobi laughed at Ashura as she rolled her eyes.

"So, let's go check out."

Ashura moved to head toward the front of the store, but stopped when she looked at the end of the aisle. A woman that she didn't know was standing at the end of it, trying had at pretending to be occupied with the description on the box she held.

"Do you know her," Nacobi asked in a low voice.

Ashura shook her head as she grabbed the basket and began moving, not paying much attention to the chic until she looked over at them out the corner of her eye. Ashura couldn't avoid her any longer.

"Do I know you?"

Danielle smirked as she placed the box back on the shelf and looked at Ashura, then Nacobi. She pushed her hands into the pocket of her jeans and shrugged her shoulders. "I don't think we've ever met."

"Well, is there a reason you over here pretending to buy things and playing peek-a-boo?" Nacobi snapped as she let her eyes move over the woman in front of Ashura, making no attempt at hiding her annoyance.

"I wasn't playing peek-a-boo, boo. That's childish. Like I said, I don't think I know either of you."

"Let me find out you tryna steal these Debbie Cakes, though."

Ashura laughed at Nacobi as she shook her head, pushing her basket around the woman so that they could get out of the store with no issues. She turned around to make sure that Nacobi was following her, and was surprised as hell when she discovered that she was. What Ashura didn't like was the way the woman was looking at Nacobi.

"Is there an issue?"

"Didn't I just say…"

"I heard what you said, but you looking at my friend as if there's an issue. You wandering the fuck around the store, just so happen to land on the same aisle as us, and now you looking my friend upside her head as if you have a problem. Something to address? Get off your chest?"

Danielle wanted to rebut, but she knew that wasn't smart being that she was for one outnumbered, and two, she was in a public place and didn't want to deal with the extra stuff that would come along with fighting in public.

"Y'all got that," she spoke, instead of acting in the initial manner that she wanted. "I don't have no issue, and I don't want no pressure. Y'all enjoy y'all night."

"Yeah, you too," Ashura tossed at Danielle's back as she walked away. "That bitch was weird."

Nacobi was standing back looking at Ashura with a smile on her face.

"What?" Ashura asked as she moved to push her cart.

"I'm just tryna see who died and made you gutta?"

"Bitch, I been about it! Especially behind you! Don't be trying to play me!"

"But who died?" Nacobi joked.

"Vince did," Ashura tossed out, causing Nacobi to laugh.

"I really just wanted you to say that."

"I know, because you petty and childish!"

"Is," Nacobi laughed as she stuck her tongue out and got in line behind Ashura.

They stood in line, their eyes scanning the store, exchanging small pieces of conversation, but their main focus was their surroundings. That's why it was so easy for Ashura to spot Anthony when he walked into the store, looking sexy as hell. Too sexy to be at the grocery store in the middle of the day.

Ashura inhaled and rolled her eyes. "Here we go."

Anthony walked up to Ashura and leaned against her basket before he looked back at Nacobi. "Y'all have to be the two most difficult women on the face of this Earth. Man, y'all don't listen to anything anyone tells you. It's like shit we say go in one ear and out the other. I said, if you needed anything to let me know, and what the fuck do y'all do?"

"We needed food," Ashura offered.

"I don't give a fuck what you need, Ashura. I told you to call me. I told you—"

"Okay, dang," Ashura snapped as they moved up the line. "How did you even know where we were anyway?"

"Come on, man. Don't ask me stupid questions. He dug into his pocket and pulled three hundred dollars off a stack and handed it to the cashier prematurely. "This for they stuff."

The cashier nodded her head and set the money to the side as she continued to ring them up.

"I don't need you to…"

Anthony shot Ashura a look that made her immediately stop talking. She pulled the basket to her as he began placing their bags in the cart.

Nacobi stood back with a smirk on her face. All that big talking Ashura did, Nacobi knew her better than anyone, and she could tell that Ashura liked Anthony more than she claimed she did. She was on the verge of saying something fly when she felt a presence behind her. She didn't need to turn around to know that it was Cole. She could smell him.

"Y'all are literally the most stalking men I know. Where did y'all even come from?"

"That's not what this is about, Nacobi. Why didn't y'all call and tell us y'all were moving?"

"We came to the store, and are about to turn right back around and go to the house once we done here. That's it."

"It doesn't matter how long you planned to be gone. Anything could happen."

"Okay, Cole!"

"Now you mad at me?"

"I'm not mad. I just said okay. Let's just drop it because I don't feel like going back and forth with you."

"Well, do what the fuck I ask you to do, and you wouldn't have to worry about that. You always got some fly shit to say. Calm all that shit down and check out so we can get back to your house. We leave for Fiji tomorrow." Cole grabbed a bag and placed it in the basket, never breaking eye contact with Nacobi.

Ashura turned to Nacobi with a knowing look on her face.

"Don't!"

Ashura nodded her head as she began to move her basket. "It's okay, Sis."

"Bitch," Nacobi mumbled.

"Aye, watch yo mouth, woman," Cole stated as he pulled her to him, placing a kiss on her cheek.

"Get off," she made a half attempt at getting him to let her go.

Once the groceries were piled into Ashura's car, they headed back to the house, unloaded them, and settled into the living room.

They sat across from one another. Cole and Nacobi stealing glances at each other. They were in a slightly better place than Anthony and Ashura. Ashura sat with her legs crossed, filing her nails down and thinking about what she wanted to cook.

"Reeves contacted us."

Ashura huffed and sucked her teeth when Anthony spoke. "Of course, he did."

"What did he say," Nacobi asked.

"He still hasn't pinpointed who is after you two, so he strongly suggests that we get off the grid."

"This is the stupidest shit I've heard in a very long time," Ashura fussed.

"Let me holla at you in the other room, Ashura."

Not giving her time to object or debate, Anthony stood and pulled her off the couch and down the hallway to Nacobi's guest room.

Nacobi looked over at Cole, who had a smile tugging at the side of his face. "You gon' cook for me?"

Nacobi placed her elbows on her knees and leaned forward. "Ashura is cooking. When were you going to tell me about Fiji?"

"I didn't want to argue with you, Nacobi. That's all we been doing, and that shit is draining. I like it better when we happy."

Nacobi felt the same way. "I know, and I'm starting to understand why you did what you did. I was just shocked, Cole. All this kind of came at me fast, and I have never had to deal with anything like this before. That's all."

Cole stood and walked over to Nacobi, sitting next to her, and pulling her close to him. "I love you."

He placed a kiss on her lips before he kissed her forehead and cheek, then kissed her lips again. Cole was about to break off the kiss until Nacobi slid her tongue into his mouth. He was engulfed in the taste of her, reaching around her to caress her ass as she moaned against his lips. His hands moved to her breast as she pressed closer to him. She missed the taste of him. The way he touched her and the way his body felt against hers. She missed everything about him.

They kissed for a while, just getting reacquainted with the taste of other until the sound of her headboard in Nacobi's guest room banging against the wall forced them apart. Before either of them could get a word out, the banging got louder.

Nacobi looked at Cole before they both burst out laughing. Nacobi crawled up the back of the couch and pressed her ear to the wall.

"Yo, what you doing," Cole chuckled. "Get down!"

"Fight back, Sis!" Nacobi yelled before she climbed down.

***

Anthony grabbed Ashura by her ponytail and moved behind her. "I'm tired of yo mouth, shawty. Always got some shit withchu!"

"Anthony, we need protection," Ashura forced out as he filled her. "Oh fuck!"

"Always snappin' back at a nigga, when all I want to do is take care of you. But you ain't used to that shit, so you wanna fight.

"You…" Ashura moaned as he moved inside of her. "You gotta get a condom.

"You need to learn to listen!"

"Okay," Ashura moaned as her knees buckled. Her head came back as Anthony gently tugged at her hair, forcing her to take all of him.

"You say okay, then the next minute you with some more fly shit. I don't like that shit, Ashura. Not at all. You gon' learn to respect me whether you want to or not. I don't care if you're older. I don't give a fuck about your past. It's me. I'm your man, and what I say goes. I don't need you fighting everything that I say to you."

Ashura felt her body tighten around Anthony as he moved inside of her. Her walls gripped him, cried for him in a way that had her juices flowing from her.

"You don't need to fight me, Ashura!"

Ashura nodded her head rapidly, grabbing the covers on the bed as the sounds of sex filled the air around them. Her body was betraying her; she didn't want to want Anthony. She didn't want to need him. She never wanted to be in the position to give anyone else her happiness. But she had to acknowledge that Anthony had a hold on her, one that she wanted to fight. One that she wanted to be released from. One that she needed.

"Uh! Anthony," Ashura groaned as she felt her orgasm creep up her spine. "Please…"

"Stop fighting me!" Anthony slapped Ashura's ass, still gripping her ponytail.

"I will."

"You don't have to fight me because I won't hurt you! I will never hurt you."

Ashura listened to him. His words penetrating her heart in a way that she knew she wasn't ready for, but she didn't have a choice. She knew that Anthony wouldn't hurt her. Her head bowed forward as she came. Her face tight, her body tense, and her soul stuck between complete happiness and past hurt. She buried her face in the pillow as her body released.

"You don't have to fight me, baby. I love you too much to ever hurt you."

12

Nacobi was in a good place, despite everything that had transpired between her and Cole. They seemed to be in a really good space.

She was dancing and singing at the top of her lungs. They were in Fiji, but the set up they had was weird. Though she was close to Nacobi, they were technically under the same roof, it was more a townhouse type set up that made them neighbors. Nacobi wasn't concerned for her friend. She knew she was good, and that was all that mattered to her. Before they landed, Anthony had sat next to Nacobi and made his intentions with Ashura crystal clear.

"I want to be with her. That's all of it."

Nacobi tilted her head to look at Anthony. "She's been through a lot of shit, Anthony. Bullshit that she didn't deserve. I want her to be happy."

"I have no intention of ever hurting her. I care about her, and whether she believes it or not, I'm not in her life to hurt her."

"Her trust is fucked off. Mine is fucked too, so I understand. You have to be patient with her.

Anthony nodded his head. "I just wanted you to know that my intentions are good."

After that talk with him, Nacobi wasn't concerned about Ashura. Anthony didn't owe her that, he didn't need to make his intentions clear to her, and the fact that he went out of his way to do so anyway gained him a lot of respect in Nacobi's eyes.

She didn't know if Cole had slept in the bed with her or somewhere else. That was just how exhausted she was when they made it in. She didn't know where anyone was, but she didn't care. All she wanted to do was get in the water that was literally right outside of her front door. She pulled her hair into a ponytail, not wanting to get it wet, before she turned and shrugged the robe off her shoulders and went to put on her swimming suit on.

"Momma taught me… not to sell work… 17-5 same color T-Shirt!" Nacobi bent over and twerked her ass as her tongue hung out of her mouth. "Ayeeeeeee," she expressed as she moved around the empty space.

She grabbed her toothbrush out of the holder and began to take care of her hygiene as Migos continued to float through the air from the Beats pill that she took with her everywhere. They had gotten in last night, but she was so jet lagged that she crashed as soon as she hit the door of the hideaway. She didn't even remember how she got inside, but after waking up this morning, she was able to take in her surroundings.

The hood raced through Nacobi's veins, never in her life had she ever laid eyes on anything as beautiful as Fiji. The water was so clear she could see to the bottom of it, so alluring and tempting, serving its purpose to perfection. She just wanted to submerge herself and forget all the bullshit she left in the states. That was what she was prepping to do now. Since waking, she hadn't laid eyes on Cole, Anthony, or Ashura. She didn't really care to look for them neither. She was dealing with her own thoughts. Her own insecurities and her own demons.

She grabbed her phone out of the pocket of her robe as it rang, thinking it was Cole and wondering how the hell she had a signal. She smiled at her screen as she realized it was none other than her mother.

"Yesssss, Victoria Naomi?"

"Nacobi, what did I tell you about the way you address me?"

Nacobi chuckled as she rolled her eyes. She would never address her mother by her first and middle name in her face, that was a no-no on so many levels. "What can I do for you, ma'am?"

"Not much, being that you are in Fiji."

Nacobi screwed her face up. "How did you know that?"

"I had a little meet up with a Mr. Cole Remington."

Nacobi literally almost swallowed her tongue. “Excuse me. What?”

“Yes, he wanted to meet both your father and I before he took you across the world.”

“What the fuck,” Nacobi whispered.

Victoria relinquished an exasperated breath. “Sometimes I wonder about you, Nacobi.”

“Ma, what are you doing having a meeting with Cole? How do you even know him?”

“I didn’t know him because you surely didn’t tell me about him. He obviously knew me because he showed up at my doorstep to speak to your father.”

“About fucking what, though?” Nacobi was annoyed, angry. She didn’t know where to direct her anger at, but she knew that Cole and her father sitting in the same room to discuss anything didn’t sit right with her.

At that moment, Cole walked into the room that they would be sharing. “Ma, I’ll call you back.”

“Hey, baby,” Cole greeted as he closed the room door and placed bags on the couch.

“Cole, why did you go to see my parents?”

Cole stopped what he was doing to give her his undivided attention. "I just wanted to meet them."

"That's something that you should have waited for me to initiate, don't you think?"

"You weren't even talking to me, Nacobi."

"I don't care, Cole. That's something that you wait for me to initiate. I don't know why you would even need to meet them."

"Nacobi, it's not a big deal, love."

"It's a big deal to me, Cole. I don't appreciate you doing things behind my back. If I wanted you to meet my parents, then I would have introduced you to them. Do you know how the dating process works?"

"I know how it works. I just wanted to speak to them about my intentions with you. Make sure they knew who I was and what I wanted from you."

"What exactly is it that you want from me, Cole?"

Cole shrugged his broad shoulders as he looked at her. "I want you. Whatever comes with you. I just wanted them to know where I stood when it came to you. That was all."

The sincerity in his voice wouldn't allow Nacobi to stay mad at him. He looked like he was scared she was about to be pissed at him again, and she didn't want to overreact yet again.

Exhaling, she walked over to him and grabbed his hands. "You can't do weird shit like that, Cole. I would have told you when I was ready for you to meet my parents. That's something that we should have talked about beforehand. I love you, and I plan to be with you, but we have to communicate with each other."

"You right, I wasn't thinking. That's my fault."

Nacobi got on her tip toes and kissed him. "Well, how did it go?"

"It went well," he said smiling, "they loved me."

Nacobi rolled her eyes and kissed him again. "Of course, they did."

13

Ashura fussed the entire jet ride. She was either too hot, too cold, uncomfortable, wanting to turn around, not needing said “protection,” or something else along the lines of extremely dramatic. They’d finally made it to the residence that they would be calling home for the next two weeks, but of course, Ashura wasn’t happy.

"You can't force me to stay here, Anthony! I don't give a fuck what you believe I need to do! I'm a grown ass woman!"

Anthony moistened his lips with a flick of his tongue. "I couldn't give two fucks about how grown you are, Ashura. I said what I said, and that's that. I don't know why you think everything I tell you is up for debate because it’s not. It never is. I told you what it was in the beginning. I'm a man, your man, whether you want to acknowledge me as that or not. What I say goes, especially where your safety is concerned. Fuck all that extra shit."

Ashura folded her arms over her chest and glared at him. "I swear you irk my fucking nerves so bad!"

"Oh well... write a note about that shit! Get it off your chest! Do what you need to do, but you are staying here, and I don't want to hear shit else about it."

Ashura huffed as she slammed the door to the room she'd been forced to live out of.

"Don't be slamming shit!"

"Fuck you!" she yelled through the door.

"I know that's what you really need. I don't know why you are depriving yourself of this premium beef. I could get you right."

"Shut up!"

"Come shut me up, Ashura!"

Behind the door, Ashura was still fuming. She didn't have any intention of being difficult, but she couldn't help to feel away about this whole ordeal. She snatched her suitcase off the ground and plopped it on the bed before she opened it.

"I'm so sick of people telling me what to do!"

Removing item after item, she stopped when she realized one of her bags were missing. She looked around the room before she held her head back, grunting and stomping her feet as she realized that her other bag was still in the living room of the beach house. She walked into the living room in search of her bag as Anthony sat in front of the television, flipping through channels. After looking around for a moment and not coming up with her bag, she stopped in front of the television, demanding that Anthony look at her.

"What?" he asked.

"Do you have my other bag?"

"What other bag?"

"The smaller pink one, Anthony. The one I distinctly remember you carrying out of the house."

Anthony grabbed a grape off the tray that was sitting beside him and popped it into his mouth. "Oh, that bag?"

"Yeah, where is it?"

"Oh," he pressed as he chewed and swallowed. "I got it."

Ashura slapped her thigh with her hand. "Okay?"

"I put that shit in a safe place where only I can find it."

"What?" Ashura snapped, not making the slightest attempt at hiding her annoyance.

"Yeah, that's your panties and bras and shit, right?"

"Yes!" Ashura crossed her arms over her chest as her anger bubbled to its max peak. "Anthony—"

"I told you to leave your panties and shit at the house before we left, but, of course, your hardheaded ass don't listen. So, I had to revert to my old ways of using extreme measures."

She didn't even stand there and go back and forth with him; she just retired to her room. She sat on the bed as a smile covered her face.

She wanted so hard to stay mad at him, but she couldn't. The scent and smell of the ocean came through her window, drawing her to it, causing her to look out. They were literally in the middle of the ocean, literally. It was so beautiful that staying in a bad mood was completely impossible. She was tired of being on guard, tired of trying to dictate the path her life took. That wasn't up to her. That was up to GOD. No one else. And whether she wanted to admit to herself in this moment or not, Anthony was a statue in her life. He wasn't going anywhere. She didn't really want him to.

She felt crazy. She wanted Anthony close, but at the same time, she wanted to be protected from him. She was lost in her own thoughts, so lost that she flinched when her bag was thrown on the bed in front of her.

"I'm warning yo lil ass now, if you put any of that shit on while in the bed with me, I'm kicking you out."

Anthony turned to walk out of the room after he spoke.

“Wait,” Ashura rushed to say. “I’m sorry about how I’ve been acting. I’m just a little all over the place.”

Anthony turned back around. “Is that why I told you that I love you, and you really didn’t say shit back? I mean, that’s cool, Ashura. I don’t have time to focus on small shit like that because I know that you will eventually love me the way that I love you.”

Ashura held her head down. “I thought you said that because we were in the heat of the moment.”

Anthony chuckled. “I don’t do fuck boy shit like that, sweetheart. If I tell you that I love you, it's solely because of what my heart feels.”

Ashura felt stupid. She wanted to tell him that she loved him too, but she didn’t know what she was feeling for Anthony. She knew she’d never felt anything like it before. She also knew that when he was around, the room felt different, the air felt stiff, and her heart did cartwheels. Even when she was pissed at him, even when she was acting crazy and not listening to him when he told her to do things. Antony was a staple. One she didn’t want to run off.

“I… care.”

“You don’t have to do that, shawty. You really don’t, and I won’t hold your failure to say it back against you. I love you. That shit won’t change, so until you get it together and can love me back, I’ll continue to love you.”

Ashura felt tears gather in her eyes, so she hid her face.

“Nacobi and Cole are in the bungalow down the ramp, I’ll be at the beach if you need me.”

With that, Anthony left the room.

14

Anthony threw pebbles into the ocean, making a solid attempt at clearing his head, and failing miserably. This was what he didn't need. He knew the moment he saw Ashura, that she would be the one to send him through some things, but nothing could prepare him for what he was facing at this moment.

Love. Well, the rejection of such a thing.

He smirked and shook his head. He was a fool for assuming he could have the things that he once fought tooth and nail against. Never met a woman that made him think of love in the manner that Ashura did. He knew she held a lot of hurt that she faced at the hands of her ex, and every day he tried with all he had to reverse those feelings.

Ashura was beyond repair. She was guarded to the max, and nothing or no one was getting through the barrier she created. He had to deal with that. First, he had to accept it, then he had to deal with it.

He reached into his pocket to retrieve his phone when it began to ring. Knowing it wasn't anyone who didn't have business to discuss. "Yo?"

"Still nothing major," Reeves updated.

Anthony exhaled. "No movement at all? Who are the motherfuckers that shot up the building?"

"We believe it to be another team, similar to Code Zero. They work in a much larger group, though."

"Facts, because the motherfuckas that was bussin' at us were far more than just two people."

"My plan is to have that taken care of before your vacation is over. What is my baby doing?"

Anthony shook his head. Reeves always referred to Nacobi as his baby but he would be a dead man if he ever said that shit to Cole. "Man, you got a death wish? You better never let Cole hear you say that shit."

"Well, now that Ashura is divorced…"

"Yeah, that will for sure get you a headshot. Not that one."

Reeves chuckled. "You sound very possessive of her."

Anthony frowned. "What the fuck you mean? She's mine! Exactly how do you expect me to sound?"

Reeves smiled on the other end of the line, recalling his initial conversation with men, and knowing that they were on the fence about the role they would play in the lives of Ashura and Nacobi. But, it seemed that they had not only found their positions, but solidified them.

"I trust you to take care of her, just be patient."

Anthony bent to grab another pebble and threw it into the ocean. "I'm trying my hardest."

"Keep trying. Hang in there, and be honest with her. They are both dealing with deep shit."

Anthony smiled. "Oh, I know."

***

Cole let out a deep sigh as he grabbed his phone. Looking over his shoulder, he assured that he was alone before he accepted the call from the unwanted caller.

"What?!"

"Have you found out anything about Vince?"

"Did I even tell your ass that I would start looking?" Cole snapped in a whisper. "Why the hell are you calling me, Danielle?"

"He still hasn't shown up, Cole. I know his wife, Ashura Trenton. She hasn't even reported him missing. I know she did something to him. I'm going to the police."

Cole exhaled. "You can't go around accusing people of shit. Give me a minute, and I'll get to the bottom of it. Send me all the information that you have on him. Just for the record, I don't give a fuck about none of this, all I want it a test when I get ready for one. I know your son ain't mine, but I want to be sure before I cut you off. Send the info, and don't call me again until I contact you."

Disconnecting the call, Cole stood. He wondered where Nacobi was, but figured she was in the water since that's what she'd been doing since they got there. He quickly grabbed his briefcase and walked into the bathroom where he set up multiple tracking devices. Some that went by voice recognition, face, hair and skin recognition, as well as thermal. All created by him, using advanced technology that the government hadn't gotten a hold of yet. He wanted to be the best at what he did, and having a background in technology helped him with his job in more ways than one.

After he had everything set up, he ran a trace on Vince. He came up with his last image being at a red light in downtown Dallas. After that, he seemed to vanish. He tapped into his GPS for that same time frame, and it showed him going home, parking his car in the garage, and never moving it again. If the murder took place at his home, then he should be able to pull the footage from the surveillance that he himself had put in place. Cole tapped into the wireless surveillance system and came up with nothing but a gray and black pixelated screen. He frowned as he tried tapping into a camera that was stationed at a different angle, and came up with the same thing.

"What the fuck," he mumbled, getting frustrated at the fact that he had somehow been outsmarted. "How did they even find these?"

Cole backtracked, dragging and dropping a picture of Ashura into the tracking software. Her movement from the last month came up. Everything from red lights, corner cameras, stores, social media. Anything she did came up on the screen. But the last thing he saw her doing was having lunch with Nacobi, picked up in the background of a picture loaded to Facebook by a couple she possibly didn't even know. When nothing came up, he traced the last person he expected to be involved, and got the shock of his life when a very damaging video began to play on his screen.

15

“What’s your favorite color?”

Good sex always relaxed Anthony, made him vulnerable and open to things that he wouldn’t normally be open to discussing. Ashura knew that this was the best time to get the intimate details of his life from him, so she took advantage.

“Red, black and white.” Anthony provided freely.

Ashura simpered against his back. He lay flat on his stomach, and Ashura rested on top of him, softly massaging his back underneath her as the sounds of the ocean echoed around them. Ashura pressed her thumbs into the lower portion of him as her hair blew into her face from the open window. She sat up straight, moving down his back so that she could massage him at a better angle, already missing the heat and comfort that being pressed against him provided.

They were fresh off a love making session that had put them both to sleep. Once they woke, they ate. Returned to the bed to go at it again, and now they had fallen into this mellow setting of just relaxing and asking each other questions that they hadn't bothered to ask before.

"What's yours?"

Ashura focused on his back, the smoothness of his skin somehow relaxing her even more than she already was. "My favorite colors are pink and turquoise."

Anthony laughed a low rumble that made her thighs shake slightly. "I knew it was about to be some girly ass colors, shawty."

Ashura shrugged, "Well, I'm a girl, aren't I?"

"That, you are."

"What's your favorite drink?"

Ashura smirked. "Hennessey."

"Word?"

Ashura nodded her head as if he could see her. "Yes. What's your favorite food?"

Anthony groaned as his mouth watered. "I love seafood. I could eat that all day with no issues. Yours?"

"I love Mexican food."

“That’s like my second favorite. Then some good ol southern food,” Anthony stated with an approving head nod. “What you like doing outside of working and shit?”

“I love reading.”

“Ohhhhhh, you be reading them nasty books, huh?”

Ashura flushed, completely guilty of indulging in the erotica genre far more than needed. “I read all types of books.”

“Like what?”

“Well, I love romance. I also love urban!”

“What’s the difference in that shit?”

Ashura rolled her eyes in her head. “Romance is about love. Pure, clean love. There may be bumps and bruises down the line, but it settles quickly. Love is the forefront. Urban is like, different. It’s about love. Love still wins, but you gon’ meet some baby momma drama, slashed tires, and shootouts before you get there. Both genres are amazing in its own right, it’s just a different route to the same thing. Love.”

Anthony smiled. “Nah, fuck that! We romance.”

Ashura laughed and shook her head.

“Who is your favorite author?”

"Oh, my GOD! Please don't ask me that because I can't answer you."

"Just try."

Ashura felt pressured. "Brenda Jackson."

"She write nasty books?"

"No, she doesn't. She writes about love. I love books like that."

"Yeah, okay," Anthony said dismissively. "Who else?"

Exhaling, Ashura spoke, "I have too many to name. Way too many to name! Then I don't want to leave anyone out, so I'll just say that I read everybody and they momma. I especially love Ivy, B. Love, Briann, Mesha Mesh, Sol, Rikenya, Genesis, Desireeeeee… um—"

"Her name Desireeeeeee," Anthony asked, mocking her.

"No, Anthony! You know it's pronounced Desiree! You just being petty!"

"Nah, I was about to say, why in the fuck would her mother name her that shit?"

She ignored him. "Then it's new authors every day, B!"

Anthony laughed at her attempt to sound gangsta.

"I literally love everyone. It's a lot! So many book baes, so little time. I'll read anyone once. If they are a great writer, then I just become a stalker. Then these authors be best sellers at like the age of sixteen, writing about love and the lack thereof. It's crazy, can you imagine knowing your calling at the age of sixteen?"

"I just wanted to fuck at the age of sixteen."

Ashura threw her head back and laughed.

"So, we might be romance with an urban twist."

Ashura grinned. "Sounds about right."

"We only got that urban twist because my dick big, and I be fucking you proper."

Ashura's jaw dropped. "Really?"

"You sit on me and tell me I don't, and I'm gon' have to flip that ass over and give you a sneak peek of this dick!"

"When did you become such a perv?"

Anthony smiled. "When you're comfortable with someone. When you love them, and know that they aren't judging everything that you do, you say and do some of the craziest shit."

Ashura regarded him silently, not prepared to dig into the topic of love just yet. Every time she thought about love, it left her in a state of depression and self-doubt.

"When is your birthday?"

Anthony stilled as she continued to massage him. Exhaling, he said, "If I tell you, you bet not get all pissed."

"Why would I get mad about you telling me your birthday, sir?"

"Because that shit in like two days."

Ashura's hands slowly came to a stop. "Stop playing, Anthony."

"Dead ass."

"That shit like in two days," she said, mocking him. "Are you serious?"

"I don't make a big deal over birthdays, ma."

"Why?" Ashura's voice was low, almost inaudible.

"I just don't."

Again, Ashura spoke in a low voice. Using extreme caution to speak on the topic of birthdays, when her own birthday was something that she tried to stay away from. "Neither do I."

"Why not?"

Ashura held her head down as her hands began moving again, only this time with a slight tremble in them that Anthony took notice of. "I used to love birthdays."

"What happened, Ashura?"

"I watched my father die, and my mother was killed as well. It um… happened at my 30th birthday party."

Anthony tried to move, to turn to her and see her face, but she wouldn't move. "Don't, Anthony."

"We don't have to talk about that."

Ashura shook her head. "No, it's okay. I think I need to talk about it."

Anthony wouldn't deny her if it was something that she wanted. He wanted to see her face, but he was okay with his position, knowing that she was close to him and he could hold her if he needed to.

"That's what made me snap, Anthony. I was leaving the house; I was fighting against myself because I was actually going to walk out and let Vince live, but he… he confessed. Told me that he had my party shot up, wanted everyone dead, including Nacobi and I. He wanted me and everyone that I loved dead." Ashura stopped speaking in order to keep her emotions together. "Sometimes I wished I would have died. I wouldn't have to deal with this pain every day. I was so lost, Anthony. I watched my dad die, and I buried my mother, but I called her, every day, every morning from the day after she died to the day that Vince confessed to having her killed. I paid the phone bill for two years, paid all the bills for two years, just to hear her voice. Just to… feel close to her. Everything I love either gets snatched from me or leaves. I. Don't know what I do wrong. It's like all the shit I did in my past is haunting me. It's like… I'm a virus or—"

"Get up!"

Ashura shook her head as a single tear slid down her face, landing on his back.

"Come on, ma," Anthony stated as he shifted upon hearing her soft sniffles turn into deep sobs.

She moved back off of him and sat on the bed, covering her face, moderately embarrassed by her breakdown.

Anthony grabbed her hands and pulled them from her face. She held her head down until he reached under her chin and made their eyes connect. "What did I tell you, Ashura? You don't need to hide from me. You don't have to fight me."

"I'm sorry."

"You sure in the hell have no reason at all to be sorry." He wiped her face with his thumbs, speeding up his pace as more tears fell from her eyes.

"I hate these shits," Anthony mumbled, his face tight as he fought hard to clear the wetness from her face. "Shit is like the worst thing ever created."

Ashura smiled through her tears as she assisted him with cleaning her face, red-rimmed puffy hazel eyes looking at him, snatching his soul in the process. He gripped her angelic face, placing kisses all over it before he pecked her lips over and over and over. Until he was content. Until her tears somehow vanished.

"You're not a virus. Not at all. You love, Ashura, you love hard, and you love deep, and sometimes that clouds your judgment of people. Vince was a predator. He saw that you loved him, made you fall in love with him, and he did this shit to you. That's why I understand you not wanting to let me in so quickly. It's hard for you, and I get it. That's why I'm patient. That's why I care about you anyway. I don't care about none of the shit you did in your past because who the fuck am I to judge you? While your parents were here, you loved them. You were a great daughter to them. That's what you remember. That's what you cherish because that's the shit that matters. Nothing else. You hear me?"

Ashura nodded her head before more tears pooled in her eyes, and before she knew it, she was crying again, but this cry was a cleanse. A cleanse that was long overdue. She felt Anthony moving, shifting to lay on his back and pulling her into his arms as she just cried. For her mother. For her father. For her loved ones that she lost. For her past. For her future. Even for Vince. She didn't know what kind of demons he was dealing with that made him the monster that he was, but she knew it had to be something deep. Unrelenting. To change him in the manner that he'd changed.

In this moment, she felt peace. GOD provided peace. The ocean provides peace. The slow, steady movements of Anthony's hand in her hair provided peace. So, she rested.

16

"I'm doing way too much," Ashura mumbled to herself as she lit the last candle in the corner of the room.

She stepped back and looked at her handiwork as a smile covered her face. If she was doing too much, she was too happy to care; she knew she was going to do something for Anthony the minute she discovered that his birthday was coming up. What better place to celebrate than in Fiji? What other person to be with than the man you love?

Yes, she loved him. Accepted that the moment he held her all night while she cried her eyes out. He didn't make it weird, didn't ask her to stop, didn't force her to "toughen up." None of that, and she quickly realized that a man who was willing to hold you down during one of your low moments, one who was willing to place his life on the line to save yours; a man of that caliber would never hurt her. More than anything she deserved love, and she wanted to love him. Only him.

Plus, she realized that she couldn't hide the fact that she was late. Her cycle was supposed to come two weeks ago, and it hadn't. She needed to communicate that to him. What if she was pregnant?

The thought made her giddy. Over the hill excited. She didn't know how Anthony would feel about it, but she hoped that if it turned out that she was pregnant, he would at least be happy. Throughout their relationship, he'd never once lied to her, never hurt her in any way, and if she was being honest with herself, she loved him. Deep. Penetrating her heart, mind, and soul.

She couldn't compare Anthony to Vince because they were worlds apart. One of them knew love, pure and unadulterated. The other… like Anthony made her realize, was a predator. Vulture. She just so happened to land on his radar.

That was her past. One she no longer cared about. One she no longer would allow to haunt her.

She smiled big, feeling extremely excited about the fact that she was about to celebrate a birthday, whether it was hers or not. She had sent Anthony to the mainland to have dinner with Cole. Cole knew what time to have him back, and that time was quickly approaching.

She had everything covered in his favorite colors; red ribbons, black and white balloons. She was dressed in a long, flowing red dress, with a big white flower tucked behind her ear, and black accessories. She was ready. Nervous, but ready.

She heard the door to the bungalow open, and heard Anthony's laugh. She could tell he was tipsy.

"Nigga, walk right!" Cole snapped.

"Aye, Ashura here?" Anthony whispered.

"Yeah, she here and waiting on you."

"Waiting on me? Shittttt I'm waiting on her! That's my baby, bruh! You bet not ever try to fuck her!"

Ashura frowned before she laughed.

"I wouldn't do that shit," Cole stated as they rounded the corner to the room. Cole took one look at the room and smiled. He looked at Ashura before he turned to face Anthony. His eyes were low, on Ashura, focusing as much as his inebriated state would allow him to. "Happy Birthday, boy! Have fun!" Cole patted Anthony on his chest. "I'll leave y'all to it." Cole walked over to Ashura and kissed her cheek.

"Aye nigga, hands and feet and big ass lips to yourself!"

Cole chuckled as he looked at Ashura. "He's all yours."

Ashura smiled. "Thanks, Cole."

"Anytime."

Cole walked out of the room, leaving the two of them alone. Anthony licked his lips before he started walking over to Ashura. "You did all this for me?" He wrapped his arms around her, his eyes low as he plucked at the flower in her hair. He smiled big before he bent down to kiss her.

"Happy Birthday," she mumbled against his lips.

"Thanks, bae." He kissed her again, gripping her ass in his hands as he lips moved over hers slowly, lazily. "You the best."

Ashura chuckled as he continued to kiss her. "I got you something."

Anthony leaned back. "How did you do all this, and you just found out that today was my birthday like two days ago?"

Ashura smiled at him. "I just… wanted to do something nice for you, so I had the boat take me to the mainland to get something made for you. It's not much…"

"It ain't gotta be much," Anthony stated with a smile tugging at his lips. "Where it's at?"

Ashura shook her head. "You gotta wait…"

"Wait?"

Ashura almost laughed at the seriousness of his face. "Yes, baby. You have to wait."

Anthony smiled big. "Oh, I'm baby and shit now? I must be doing something right."

"You do a lot right."

Anthony felt his chest swell. "Is that right?"

Ashura nodded her head, aware of him in a way that made her smile just because she was in his presence. "I love you, Anthony. I was scared to get to that point with you because I didn't know what would happen if I opened my heart to another. The last time I did, I was taken advantage of, but the way you touch me. The way you look at me and address me. I know that you care about me too much to ever hurt me, and that knowing makes me love you. Deep . I fought it, trust me when I tell you I fought it, but I'm tired of that and want to love you securely. I don't care about caution. You can't love with caution."

"You will never need to," Anthony stated in a soft voice. "Not with me. Never."

Ashura nervously pushed her hair out of her face, watching him.

"I love you too, high yella."

Ashura rolled her eyes before she kissed him.

"I know that you do and I feel blessed. I want to celebrate your birthday, but you have to wait on your gift."

"So, what we doing? You cooked for me?"

"I did, but I didn't do much, I figured you ate already."

"With Cole," Anthony let out. "Nah, I had a coupla drinks though. Nigga is feeling good, but I didn't eat like that, so I'm hungry."

She realized then that he never had her cooking before. That fact made her even more nervous. "Ummm, I could…"

"Nah, I'll just eat bigger portions of what you made."

"But, you don't even know what I made."

"Shitttttt, if I don't get full, then I'll just eat you 'til I am. Either way, I won't go to bed hungry! No child left behind, Ashura!" Anthony laughed as he leaned back on the bed, looking over at her out the side of his eye. "You look good as fuck."

Ashura blushed as she moved to go get the food she prepared. She ran her hands down the front of her dress, relieving them of the perspiration that had gathered there. She felt like a school girl about to go on a date with her first crush after admiring him from the shadows forever. She lingered in the kitchen, trying to gauge the time she had, and questioning if she had time to make something else. She didn't want him to think that she couldn't cook, when it was something that she loved to do. What she had for him was a smaller prepped combination of hand foods; chips, cheese, crackers, grapes, and California Spring Rolls.

"That's the stupidest combination ever! He might not even like sushi! Why would I make sushi?" she mumbled to herself as she began to panic. "Fuck my life, I swear," she let out as she peeked around the corner, as if she could see the room from the kitchen area when it was clear across the bungalow. "Maybe, he'll just fall asleep if I stay in here long enough."

Anthony was on the verge of falling asleep until he heard Ashura moving around in the kitchen. He pulled himself from the bed and slowly made his way to the kitchen where he found her pacing. He frowned before he rubbed his hand down his waves, smiling as he listened to her mumble to herself.

"What you doing, Ashura?"

Ashura flinched as she turned to look at Anthony. "Um…"

"What happened to the food?"

Ashura deflated, defeated. "Okay, so look…"

Anthony crossed his arms over his chest, entertained by her giddiness. He always liked when she was a little less than perfect.

"I didn't cook. I know how to cook, and I love doing it, but I… I haven't cooked like food *food*."

"I'm lost, sweetheart. What did you make?"

"Well, you said you liked seafood."

"I do."

"So, I made sushi."

Anthony frowned as he looked at her. “Fuck you mean you made sushi?”

Ashura covered her face. “I knew this was stupid!”

“I was wondering why I didn’t smell shit up in here cooking.”

“The supplies are limited and…”

“Where it's at?”

“I'm not used to cooking for…”

“Black people?”

“Not… no! I just always made stuff like this. Things that are on the healthier side.”

“Where the catfish at?”

Ashura’s face was red with embarrassment. “I don’t know how to make catfish.”

“The fuck,” Anthony almost shouted. “You don’t know how to make catfish? What about shrimp alfredo? Lobster? Crawfish! Crab! Shit…do you know how to make hush puppies?”

“I don’t know what hush puppies are.”

Anthony leaned against the counter dramatically. “What?” he hushed in a low, over dramatized voice. “Yo ass can't make hushpuppies. That’s disrespectful as fuck!”

“This is horrible,” Ashura mumbled.

“Please tell me you know how to deep fry some shit! Do you use seasoning salt? Do you wash your meat before you cook it? Do you cook it first then season it? Please tell me you know how to use more than salt and pepper. Please tell me you know how to make your ribs tender. Do you make ribs? How many cheeses you be putting in your mac and cheese?”

“I use four che—”

“That’s too much got damn cheese,” Anthony exclaimed as he threw his hands up.

Ashura placed her hands on her hips, at her breaking point with his ridicule. “You have to understand.”

Anthony held his head back and closed his eyes before inhaling. “You right.” He moved to wrap Ashura in his arms as his face set in a deep pout. “We gotta take you to the hood, shawty. A nigga like me needs catfish.”

“Have you ever tried Sushi?”

“Nah, I ain't tried it, but I'm willing to try it for you.”

“Really?” Ashura beamed.

“Yeah, where is it?” Anthony was too caught up in her to continue to bash her cooking. If she prepared anything for him, he would try it. At least once.

Ashura got on her tip toes to kiss him before she moved around the small island in the kitchen and separated the cover from the tray holding the food she prepped. She bit her lower lip nervously as she grabbed a few of the rolls and placed them on a plate.

"Why that shit transparent?"

Ashura hadn't heard Anthony move, but he was standing over her shoulder. His full attention was on the roll, which didn't look appetizing at all to him.

"It's not transparent, its sticky rice. Just try it," Ashura prodded as she turned to him with a roll in her hand, placing it to his lips.

Anthony leaned back as if he were in the Matrix. "Whoa."

Ashura laughed as she stuck her hand out further, causing him to move as if he was Neo and getting shot at by an agent. Ashura moved her hand to follow him for a moment before she gave up. "This is childish."

"Take me slow," Anthony stated as he placed his hands on the side of her, pinning her against the island.

Ashura huffed and leaned her head to the side, sticking the roll out to him. Anthony bit into it, making a face that reflected disgust before he relaxed a little, chewing the roll slowly, testing its taste against his tongue while drunken eyes stayed connected with Ashura's hopeful ones.

Once he was done chewing, he smirked at Ashura. “That wasn’t that bad.”

“Seeeee.”

“Shit still ain't no catfish, though. You still going on a trip through the hood. You gon’ come back making catfish plates.”

17

Nacobi smiled as she held the cards in her hands close to her face, peeking over them at Cole as he focused on the hand he was dealt.

“I can't get a book with this,” Cole grumbled as he threw down a heart that he knew for sure Nacobi would cut.

Nacobi quickly cut him.

“This is bullshit! This is why two person Spades is stupid. It can only go one way.”

“I asked you if you wanted to play GoFish.”

“I don’t know how to play that childish game, Nacobi. But Spades is stupid with two people only.”

“It's only stupid to you because you losing.”

Cole released a few incomprehensible curse words before he returned to looking at his hand. He leaned back in his seat and looked at Nacobi, who was enjoying his defeat a little too much for his liking.

"I quit!"

Cole stood from his seat and threw his hand down before he walked off. Laughing, Nacobi got up from her seat and followed him, wrapping her arms around his waist as he walked into the bedroom.

"I can't believe you're a sore loser!"

"I'm not! You just in there taking advantage of the situation."

Nacobi sat on the edge of the bed as Cole moved to walk into the closet and began shuffling through his multiple layers of black linens. Nacobi eyed him, the frown adorning his face not doing anything to negate his handsomeness.

"What are you doing?"

Cole looked over at her. "Get dressed. Wear something simple."

Nacobi frowned. "What?"

"Something simple, loose preferably, so I can watch your ass jiggle when you walk. Oh, did you bring that light blue sun dress you had hanging in your closet?"

"Cole…"

"I made reservations."

Nacobi's face scrunched up before he slapped her forehead with her hand. "You suck at dating, Cole."

Cole was authentically confused. "How?"

"You don't go from kicking it; I mean, I wasn't even thinking about going out. I have on pajamas."

"We in Fiji, Nacobi! We can't stay in the bungalow forever. I was trying to do something nice for you."

"But most times when guys do that, it's known or at least hinted at. This is random as hell!"

Cole stepped out of the closet, disorientation covering his face as a plain black v-neck shirt hung from his hand. "I just wanted to take you out."

Why did he have this pull on her? Why couldn't she be mad at him or fight him? Why was she now feeling bad about the fact that he was springing this on her out of nowhere? His eyes. Dark. Penetrating. Wouldn't allow her to press him much at all.

"But you should have told me or at least said, 'Bae, I have plans for us later.' I don't know. Something. Maybe I'm overreacting. I'll get dressed."

Cole stood cemented, ambiguity apparent in his gaze as he looked at her. He watched her as she got off the bed, removing the band from her hair and allowing it to fall with a huff of frustration. Oblivious to the discomfort he'd placed Nacobi in, or any woman that gets a date sprung on them, he followed behind her slowly. His eyes set in a doleful expression as he allowed them to scene her.

"We ain't gotta go, shawty. I can cancel the date. I was just… trying to do something nice."

Nacobi looked over at him as she plugged in her flat irons. "It's fine, Cole. We can go. You're right, we in Fiji. Can't sit and do nothing all day, even though I've been enjoying you."

"I'm enjoying you too," Cole confessed. "Just wanted to see your ass in a dress, put you on the back of my bike and take you to eat."

"Bike," Nacobi fussed.

Cole smiled. "Yes."

"I ain't getting on no bike, Cole," Nacobi stated with finality as she unplugged the flat iron.

Cole's face dropped. "Whatchu mean you're not getting on? It's the only thing I have."

"Most men rent cars, limousines, hell even buses, but you got a whole bike to go on dates, but what you telling me is that you got a motorcycle? You want me to get on that motorcycle with a sundress on?"

"I gotta be able to…"

"See my ass jiggle," Nacobi finished. "But you'll be driving, so I don't understand what the point is."

"When you get off, I'll be able to see it."

Nacobi bounced on the bed when she flopped down on it. "Okay, well you can your clothes off and see this ass in action up close and personal because I am not getting on the back of no bike. I don't have time to die in Fiji."

"I wouldn't let that happen." Cole's voice was so deep and serious.

Nacobi rolled her eyes. "I was being sarcastic."

Cole relaxed. "Well, you should trust me to keep you safe. All I do is drive bikes. I know how to control one, and I won't go too fast." Cole smirked as he looked at her. "Every time you tell me to slow down, I do it. Right?"

Nacobi threw her head back as butterflies caused her stomach to flutter. "Yes."

Cole leaned forward, placing both of his hands on the bed beside her. As he got close to her face, Nacobi brought his face down to look into his dark eyes. The sexual tension between them… thick. She didn't understand why they weren't fucking right now. Cole looked into her eyes, knowing what she wanted and fighting against his need to accommodate her.

He leaned in, brushing her hair behind her ear, his eyes roaming her face. "I know what you want. I want it too, but it's all we've been doing. I want to get you out, watch the wind blow through your hair. Watch you take in the other people around us. Watch your eyes get big when something weird happens. I want to see you outside of this room. Then, I'll fuck you. Long. Hard. Soft. Slow. Whatever you want. You down?"

Nacobi inhaled. "You should have led with that shit."

Cole laughed before he kissed her lips before he moved back.

***

Nacobi swore she would die. She knew it was over for her the moment Cole sat her on the bike.

"I'm so scared."

Cole grabbed the spare helmet from behind her before he smiled at Nacobi, his head angled to look at her. "We just went through this."

Nacobi pulled her jacket together before she exhaled. "I don't care what we went through already. I'm still scared."

"You don't need to be scared. I told you I got you."

Nacobi swallowed and bowed her head. "I know. I just—"

Cole lifted her head to look into her eyes. "I got you, Nacobi. Always."

Nacobi looked into his eyes, knowing he was serious before she mumbled, “I know. Okay.”

Cole pushed her hair over her shoulder before he gently slid the helmet over her head. He smiled at her and the frown she assumed he couldn’t see that covered her face. He peeled the mask of the helmet back before he leaned in and kissed her.

“Stop frowning.”

Cole placed his helmet on his head before he mounted his bike. Nacobi admired him, all black everything covering his light skin, tattoos, and the helmet made him extremely alluring. Again, she wondered why he wasn’t inside of her.

Cole pulled his mask down before he turned to look at her. “Grab me.”

Nacobi’s eyes rounded. “I can hear you.”

“You have a mic in your helmet. If you get uncomfortable at all, let me know. I’ll stop. Slow down. Whatever you need.”

Nacobi reached around him, linking her fingers together in front of his stomach. Holding him tight. Cole felt her scoot closer to him, her breasts pressed against his back, and he turned the key to the bike. Immediately, Nacobi gripped him tighter.

“Relax, Nacobi.”

Nacobi closed her eyes as she leaned into him. His voice was soothing, easing her fear slightly before he pulled off. Nacobi had her eyes closed tight, gripping him even tighter. Her legs clenched around him as he merged onto the bridge that would lead them over the water.

"Open your eyes," Cole coaxed. "Look at how beautiful the ocean is at night."

"Nope, nigga. I don't care about the water."

"Baby," Cole laughed.

"I can't open my eyes. I feel like I'm about to have a panic attack. Stop talking to me. Just drive."

Cole shook his head as they cleared the bridge, making it to the small track that covered the shore and led to the main road that would guide them to their destination. It wasn't that he didn't put any thought into their date because he did. He just didn't realize that he needed to let Nacobi in on his plans. He didn't want it to be a surprise; the notion of telling Nacobi was an afterthought, something that he would try to never do again. He could admit that he didn't know much about dating. Fact was, Nacobi was the first woman that he'd entertained beyond sex. She had quickly developed into an addiction for him.

It wasn't a matter of if she would be in his life or how long. It was a matter of, how long before he messed up. Did something else that she considered imbecilic. He was a man. One who knew how to express himself, and he had no issues being that man. Putting his foot down, shutting Nacobi down when need be. Most times, he allowed her to talk. Let her vent. Let her get whatever frustration she had at the moment out.

"This isn't that bad."

Cole focused on the road ahead of him. "I told you it wouldn't be."

"Why don't you like driving your car?"

"I don't like small spaces."

"So, what do you plan to do when your old and can't operate a motorcycle?"

"I plan to have you driving me around wherever I need to go."

Nacobi smiled as she held him tighter. "I'm down for that."

18

Cole walked up behind Nacobi and swooped her up in his arms, causing her to squeal.

"Cole!"

Cole kissed her cheek as he placed her back on her feet. "I love you."

Nacobi turned around and kissed him. "I love you too. Thank you for dinner."

"Thank you for wearing this dress."

Nacobi turned around and looked at the bike that they rode in on. She was no longer scared to be on the back of it, not if Cole was driving. He knew what he was doing and was so got damn sexy when he was doing it. "Are you ready?"

Cole smiled as he picked up her helmet and placed it on her head. "Oh, you ready now huh?"

"I'm a rider," Nacobi stated matter of factly as she threw her leg over the bike, settling on the back of it before it began to shift, leaning with her on it. "Oh shit!"

Cole caught her, the bike and his helmet before any of them could hit the ground. Nacobi was holding on to the bike for dear life as Cole pulled it back upright. He smiled at the wideness of her eyes.

"I almost busted my ass."

Cole shook his head as he pulled her mask down and straddled the bike, putting his helmet on. Nacobi wrapped her arms around him as soon as he was settled. Cole took off in the direction of the beach. The night air engulfing them as he cruised the coastline, seeing the bungalows in the distance.

Nacobi was feeling the wine that she drank at the restaurant. She bit her lip behind her mask before she released a sigh.

Cole, who was on always on alert, turned his head slightly. "You good?"

Nacobi nodded her head. "I'm straight." She allowed her voice to drop before she continued speaking. "Pussy just wet, Cole."

Cole turned his head again before returning his attention to the road. "Is it?"

Nacobi unhooked her hands and slide one over his dick. She heard him groan before the motorcycle slowed slightly. "That type of shit will have us getting locked for indecent exposure, Nano."

Nacobi moved her hand to work past the button of his jeans. "I told you I'm a rider."

Cole pulled over to the side of the road, behind a boulder of rocks, that literally sat off the shore of the ocean. Literally a mile from where they took residence. Turning the car off, he pulled Nacobi's hand from his jeans. "Get up here."

Nacobi didn't waste a minute before she was climbing off the bike. Climbing back on it, facing him. She went to remove her helmet but his voice stopped her.

"Don't."

Nacobi's hands stilled at the bottom of her helmet as she watched Cole through the tint of her mask. He removed his jacket and sat it behind her before he reached around her. She heard the beginnings of something soft began to play in her ear. It took her a minute to make out what it was but once the voice came through she knew immediately. The melody, along with the sound of the ocean had her ready. Beyond ready. "Make Love" by SILK played as Cole reached out to caress her breast.

Cole wrapped his arm around her to pull her closer, standing slightly to remove his member before he settled again. Nacobi wrapped her arms around his neck before she reached down to lift her dress up.

"Slow."

Nacobi nodded, her eagerness not subsiding at all. Her movements bordered on being frantic.

"Nano." Cole gripped her hand and placed it on his dick. Its thickness, fullness making Nacobi eager, even the more. "Slow."

Nacobi lifted, placing Cole at her entrance as she slid down on him, slowly as he ordered.

They both released groans the moment their bodies touch intimately.

"Always so fucking wet," Cole let out as his eyes lowered, looking at Nacobi as her head went back. She worked her hips against him, her hands clenching his shoulders as she fought to get closer.

"Umm fuck." Her whimper echoed in Cole's ears as if it had been shouted through a microphone.

"You my rider right," Cole asked as she worked against him. "Ride me. Let me see that shit."

Nacobi felt him deep inside of her and nothing that she could attempt to form into words would describe the feeling of Cole Remington. His hands moved over her in a way that reflected his heart, his breathing- labored and catching due to being inside of her. The way her name slipped from his lips ever so often when she pushed hard against him.

His discovery was the furthest thing from his mind. He only wanted to feel her, in this moment.

Cole removed her helmet before he removed his own, watching her eyes dance to find his before her lips clashed against his at the same time that the waves of the ocean collided with the boulder.

"Fuck me, Nano," Cole coached as he gripped her ass in his hands, guiding her onto him. Forcing his tongue into her mouth, giving to her just as much as he was taking. Her vaginal muscles gripped him as much as they could, making him aware of how wet she was. How tight. How perfect.

Her rhythm against him broke, her tempo thrown off by the greeting of her orgasm. "Please! Cole!"

"Cum for me!"

"Please! Please! Fuck!"

She was begging for something that he was freely giving to her.

Nacobi's entire body tensed before it began to quiver uncontrollably around him. Her orgasm was charged, sending her body into overdrive with him still tapping depths inside of her.

They made love near the shore of the beach, as if they were in the comfort of their own dwelling and they didn't stop until they were both content.

19

Two weeks in Fiji gave both Nacobi and Ashura a clear mind and a fresh tan. Ashura had developed a huge obsession with Anthony. Everything he did and said, she clung onto it and he always delivered. Never dropped her or let her down. Pain and Anthony didn't equate in anyway and she loved him.

She smiled at the thought.

"Yo face gone break," Nacobi mumbled as they climbed out of Ashura's car to attend the third meeting they had since returning. Ashura was trying to find a new office space for her firm and so far, they hadn't come with anything that she loved.

"I'm happy," Ashura declared. "Can't I be happy?"

Nacobi closed her door and looked at her friend over the top of the car. "Of course, you can! I've never saw you this happy before."0

Ashura grabbed her purse out the back seat before she stood back up, giving her friend a half smile as she closed her car door. "You've never saw it on me because I have never been this happy. Never."

They two ladies walked into the building, chatting in low tones before they reached the lobby where the person they were meeting with was supposed to be stationed. They were a few minutes early so they took a seat and waited. "So, how are things with Cole?"

Nacobi blushed. "Amazing. You know when you deal with a lot of bullshit then you finally meet a guy that has a pure heart and good intentions, it's hard to not be judgmental. But with Cole, I don't give a fuck no more. I don't know if the dick is clouding my judgment or what but I don't care about his past, he doesn't care about mine. He genuinely wants me happy and I want the same thing for him. So that's my baby. He everything and I wish a bitch would."

Ashura giggled at her best friend as she looked around the lobby to see if she had gotten anyone's attention. Luckily the lobby was empty. She glanced down at the watch on her wrist before she looked around the lobby.

"Whoever this woman is, she is late as hell."

Nacobi glanced at her watch as well. "Yeah, we were early so I thought I was trippin but nah, this heffa just late."

Ashura grabbed her phone, about to call the person that they were supposed to be meeting with but she saw a woman walk out from the back, speaking to a woman.

One that both Nacobi and Ashura immediately recognized as the one that was at the grocery store acting weird as hell before they left for Fiji.

"Ain't that the bit..."

"Yeah, that's her," Ashura confirmed as she stood. "Why the fuck she keep poppin up?"

Nacobi saw the flash of heat past through her friend's eyes and knew she was on the verge of snappin. "Calm down, killa."

"I just wanna know who the hell she is. I don't know why she keeps "coincidently" poppin up everywhere we are. I'm annoyed by her ass."

"It was just two times though."

"Two times too many," Ashura mumbled as they waited for the woman to approach them. They seemed to get the attention of ol girl before they grabbed the attention of the woman that they were there to meet.

Danielle smirked as she turned to Stacy Mann, the woman that would be handling the investigation of the disappearance of Vince. Stacy was in the midst of moving her office downtown so she assumed that was why Ashura Trenton was there. Looking to move into this space once Stacy was gone.

"Fuck is this bitch smirking like that for? Look," Ashura stated with a snap of her neck and a roll of her hands, "I don't have time for this. I'm about to ask her straight up what her issue is."

"She already told you that she didn't know us when we were at the grocery store."

"I need her to run that back to me, just to be on the safe side."

Ashura dropped her coat over her arm as she walked over to the two women with Nacobi right behind her. She gave Danielle a fake, forced smile as she turned to look at the two of them.

"Hello. I have a meeting with you, Stacy. I know that we are a little early…"

"Yes, Mrs. Trenton, I was just wrapping up with my new client and I was going to be right with you."

Ashura nodded her head. "Right, um…I actually came over here to meet your client. It seems that we continue to run into each other and I never seem to catch her name."

Stacy smiled, completely unaware of the tension between the ladies. "Oh, this is Danielle C—"

"Nice to meet you," Danielle stated, reaching her hand out to shake Ashura's. Ashura made her fake smile wider as she nodded her head, not bothering to reach out and shake Danielle's hand.

Danielle pulled her hand back with a suck of her teeth. "Well, I guess everyone wasn't raised to have manners."

"No," Ashura stated as she continued to smile. "I was raised to have manners, I just don't shake the hands of peasants. That's all boo."

Nacobi laughed as she watched the exchange between the two ladies. "Boss Bitch."

Danielle looked at Nacobi and fought not to roll her eyes. She knew Nacobi was the woman that Cole was with, and that fact made her dislike Nacobi even the more. She had plans for Cole, plans that included her and their son being the family that she always wanted them to be, but she knew that she had to get rid of Nacobi first.

"Um… you're here to see the office space, correct?" Stacy felt the need to interject and say.

"Yeah, if I recall that was what we were meeting about."

Stacy nodded her head. "Of course, Danielle if there wasn't anything else that you needed, I would like to take care of Ms. Trenton."

Trenton, Danielle thought. *Hmmm, the bitch didn't isn't even looking for her husband! Just dropped his last name and on to the next dick! Trenton.*

"Of course," she cooed as she moved to walk away from the group. "Can you call me as soon as your settled in regard to that very important business matter."

Stacy nodded her head. "Of course."

Danielle mugged Ashura and Nacobi as she walked off.

"Watch yo eyes little momma," Ashura warned.

"Don't speak to me bitch," Danielle snapped.

Ashura didn't even allow the last syllable to leave Danielle's lips before she was snatching her back by her hair. She watched as she slid across the marble floors, surprised shrieks coming from everyone that was watching the scene unfold.

Danielle was off the floor in a flash and charging Ashura before she could prepare. They both fell to the ground, Danielle landing on top of Ashura before Ashura flipped them over and began to go to work on her face.

"Oh, my GOD," Stacy exclaimed. "Get her off of her!" She was addressing Nacobi, but Nacobi was too busy making sure Danielle not at any point started to get the best of Ashura.

Stacy made a move to try and break up the fight but Nacobi released a malicious chuckle that had her stopping in her stance. "Don't do that, sweetie. It's just not smart. Let her get that shit out then we can move on."

“This bitch disrespectful,” Ashura snapped as she continued to slam her fist into Danielle’s face. Her rage made her blind, all she could see was blood until Nacobi was pulling her off a near unconscious Danielle.

“Let’s get the hell out of her before they call the police on us,” Nacobi groaned as she pulled Ashura out of the doors of the building.

***

“Ow,” Ashura winced as Anthony stuck her swollen hand in a bucket of ice water. His annoyance was written all over his face as he looked from the bucket to her face, shaking his head then looking back down at the bucket.

“I’m sorry,” she mumbled.

“Stop talking, ma.”

“She called me out of my name and I…”

“I don’t care what the fuck she called you. You don’t fight random bitches in public. That shit is not cute.”

“I wasn’t trying to be cute, I was trying to break that bitch face.”

Anthony looked at Ashura and couldn’t contain his smile. Her face was so soft, so gentle, so innocent. But behind that face, behind that cool and calm demeanor was a savage waiting to be activated. Waiting to be tampered with. Waiting to be awakened.

"I don't want you fighting, Ashura."

"I haven't had a fight in so long. I was there on business. I was there to look at the space for the office, nothing else but she came at me sideways and I couldn't just let that slide. You allow people to disrespect you once and all they will do it continue to disrespect you. I've tolerated enough disrespect to last a lifetime."

"Who was this woman?"

"I don't even know her. Nacobi and I ran into her at the grocery store then again at the law office. Outside of that, I never saw her before that."

"If you don't know her and only ran into her twice then why you was beefin for her like that?"

"Her vibe is off," Ashura accessed. "She just gives off this aura like she knows us but every time I ask her if she does, she says that she doesn't. She apparently has a case that the Stacy lady that I was there to meet that would handle for her."

"What's this chic's name?"

"Donna, Danielle or…Danielle is her name. I swear bae, this chic is weird as hell."

Anthony stopped massaging Ashura's hand to look back at her. "Danielle what?"

"Huh," Ashura asked, looking down at her hand, trying to wiggle it to prompt him to keep massaging.

"What's her last name?"

"I didn't get it; I was too busy fucking her face up."

In order for things to stay settled, Anthony continued to massage Ashura's hand. He knew the Danielle that Ashura and Nacobi were encountering had to be the same one that had miraculously reappeared in Cole's life. He was sure about that because he knew that Danielle was also fucking Vince. But, what did she want with Ashura?

20

Danielle was tired of living in the shadows. She knew something happened to Vince and after investigating a little further, she knew that Ashura Trenton had something to do with it. After her last encounter with Ashura and Nacobi, she knew she had to pin this murder on them. It was the only way she would be able to put them away for good.

She was so determined to have both of them under the jail that she wouldn't stop before she got it done. After her last encounter with the two, more so Ashura, everything about her life had been in a disarray. She was running out of money and her appearance, bruises left on her by Ashura, didn't make her very alluring so that she could do what she usually did to make a living. She couldn't believe she attacked her at the law office. Ashura was a smaller woman, petite and slim, but she was strong and it was clear to Danielle that she could defend herself. She wasn't sure why Ashura allowed Vince to beat her ass because obviously, she could have gotten back with him.

She didn't see Vince as an abuser because he never hit her, never even raised his hand to her. He loved her, respected her and treated her like a queen. That was why she was so patient with him in his process of divorcing Ashura, she wanted everything that he was offering. She still did.

Over the years of being with Vince, Danielle became accustomed to a certain lifestyle, even though she now knew it was Ashura's money that was being splurged on her, she didn't care. She didn't owe Ashura anything and Danielle's greed for money wouldn't allow her to feel sorry for Ashura.

Pinning Ashura Trenton for the disappearance of Vince Combs was her main agenda. It was all she wanted to get done, and it was something that she wouldn't rest on until it was done.

She climbed out of her car and walked up the breezeway to the beautiful two story house that seemed to have been abandoned. The eerie feeling, she got when she walked up to the doorway, crept up her spine. She peeked over her shoulder before using her key to enter the house. This wasn't her first time being here, in fact, she's been to Vince and Ashura's place a number of times. She even fucked Ashura's husband in her bed.

A mischievous smirked covered her face at that thought. She knew the danger she was putting herself in with digging into this situation, but she was in too deep to care.

She opened the door and walked into the foyer. Her eyes are taking the room in as she walked deeper into the room.

Everything was spotless. Clean from top to bottom.

Suspiciously clean.

Everything was still in place and there was absolutely anything that spoke to her case of foul play.

She started in the living room, lifting up pillows on the couch and looking under them, opening cabinets and closet doors before she stormed up the stairs. She continued her search, coming up with absolutely nothing.

Frustrated and annoyed, Danielle left out of the house with the same exact thing that she came in with. Nothing.

Once she was back inside of her car, her phone began to ring.

"Hello?"

"Is it true?"

"What?" Danielle snapped in confusion. "Who is this?"

"Reign! Danielle…is it fucking true? You have my son?"

Danielle's heart dropped, the wind leaving her body causing it to slump against the seat. "Wha… Reign? How did you get…"

"That shit don't matter! Is your son mine?!"

***

Cole sat back in his seat, sulking.

"You just need to talk to her."

"I don't want to talk to her, Anthony. I want her to fucking talk to me."

Anthony shook his head and inhaled. "You've been in love with that woman for a very long time. I think the fact that she was able to get something past you is the thing that's bothering you the most."

Cole agreed. "That. Plus, the fact that the shit she does can land her in jail for the rest of her life. I can't afford that shit."

"I understand that." Anthony took a pull from his blunt and exhaled. "I think Ashura ass is pregnant."

Cole's head snapped towards his best friend. "For real? How you figure?"

"I know her body. She ain't had her cycle since before we left for Fiji."

Cole smiled. "Damn, congratulations bruh.

"Thanks," Anthony spoke absently. "I don't know for sure yet. I'm waiting on her ass to tell me."

Cole smiled, he knew his friend was nervous about the possibility. “Speaking of babies…”

Anthony looked at Cole. “What?”

“Danielle’s baby is Reign’s.”

Anthony choked on the smoke that was floating from his lungs. “What the fuck? She was fucking Reign too?”

Cole laughed. “Yup!”

“How you find that out?”

Cole smirked. “I have my ways.”

“Sneaky ass nigga.” Anthony laughed and shook his head. His thoughts went back to Cole and his situation with Nacobi. “Say man, answer me this.”

“Shoot.”

“Why do you think you are the way that you are with Nano?”

“Whatchu mean?”

Anthony kissed his teeth. “Come on, bruh”, he pressed as he took a pull from his blunt. “You been knowing shawty for a long ass time.”

Cole shook his head. “I didn’t know her.”

“But you’ve seen her before.”

"Come on, Cole. You literally tried to convince yourself that you didn't know her. I let you do that shit because I knew you were dealing with something deeper but now, that's your shawty. You need to tell her."

"Fuck no", Cole spat.

"You knew her…"

"I didn't". Cole cut in.

"You watched…"

"I saw enough of her. Part of my arrangement was to not get attached, and to keep my distance. I failed like a motherfucka at that first part. I was never supposed to have a conversation with her ass. Then she hit me with her car and shit, spoke to me and it didn't even matter that she was cursing my ass out. I just…couldn't stay in the shadows any longer. That in itself was driving me crazy."

"Hell, yeah it was", Anthony agreed, "you were contemplating capping shawty."

Cole dropped his head, realizing how dumb that idea was. "Stupidest shit ever, bruh."

"You sacrificed a lot for her."

Cole nodded his head. "I'll do that shit all over again too."

Anthony went to speak when his phone rang. He glanced down at it, seeing that he had an incoming call from Reeves, he answered via the speaker.

"Speak."

"It's handled."

Anthony glanced over at Cole. "Who was it?"

"Snake and Rambo from the Operation Union."

"What the fuck," Cole whispered.

"I was just calling to let you guys know that they have been taken care of indefinitely. As of right now, the coast is clear."

"Bet."

"Until next time Code Zero."

Cole shook his head. "Code Zero has officially retired."

21

Nacobi closed out of the multiple screens she was in on her laptop before she stretched her arms and legs out. She was going stir crazy looking at the screen of her computer. Since she was back in the states, it was back to business as usual. She wasn't going to pick up with her cleaning service just yet, but she was itching to get back into the swing of things. As long as Cole didn't know what she was doing, she knew she'd be good. She just needed to be extra careful, sure to cover all her tracks like she always did.

Speaking of Cole, he'd been distant since they came back from Fiji. She'd only seen him a total of two times, though they'd been back for weeks. Both times she saw him, all they did was have sex before he disappeared again. Everything he did was suspicious to her.

For the last three years, she had been investigating the murder of her grandfather and coming up with nothing. Her father gave her this bullshit story about a "gambling deal gone bad" but she never believed that. Never trusted her father to tell her the truth about what happened to him. So, she tried to find answers on her own, and recently, she ran across an image of two men, ones with the build of

Anthony and Cole, but she didn't want to assume. So, she asked her father, who declined to give her any information about the situation.

After running into brick wall after brick wall, she finally decided that she would flat out ask Cole if he had anything to do with it. But, she had to get him to be in her presence first.

Nacobi leaned back in her seat and exhaled as she looked over the spreadsheet in front of her. For some weird reason, the thrill of being a cleaner was gone. She hadn't worked since Vince, and when she was in Fiji, she didn't think about the crazy career she had left in Texas. Now, she was back in the face of reality, and the reality is, she was in a different place.

She grabbed her phone to call Cole. Biting her lip and shaking her leg as the phone rang.

"Hello?"

"Hey, baby," Nacobi greeted.

"Wassup," Cole responded, dryly.

Nacobi leaned back, removing her phone from her ear and looking at it before she placed it back on her ear. Deciding not to overreact, she inhaled then exhaled to relax. "Were you still going to come by later on today?"

Cole looked through his car window, up at Nacobi's parent's house, the house he had been sitting outside of for the last hour. "Nah, I had something come up but I plan to see you soon."

The way he made that statement had Nacobi wondering what he meant by that. "Ok…"

"Yeah, I got some shit to handle. I'll try to swing by and see you tomorrow."

Nacobi swallowed hard. "Cole, is everything okay? You've been kind of distant since Fiji. I don't know what I did but I…"

"You good, Nacobi," Cole insisted. "It's good. We good. I'm just dealing with some shit right now, getting to the bottom of some things but if you need me for anything, don't hesitate to call me."

Nacobi was having a hard time understanding why he was cold towards her. He was talking to her as if she was a client of his, someone he was doing business with versus making love to. "Why are you speaking to me as if I'm getting on your nerves or some shit?"

"That's not what I'm doing," Cole declined.

"What the fuck do you call it?"

"What I tell you about your mouth, Nacobi?! Stop talking to me any kind of way!"

"What the fuck you mean, Cole?! What's up with you?"

"You think you run shit!"

"I don't think…"

"You always got some fly shit to say! How many times do I have to ask you to respect me? I'm not that wack ass nigga you used to. Watch yo fucking mouth!"

Nacobi's eyes were as big as saucers. "Cole, what the hell is…"

"Nothing." Cole ran a hand down his face as the person he came to see, climbed out of his car and walked up the driveway to his home. "I love you and I'll talk to you later."

Not waiting for her to respond, Cole disconnected the call and climbed off his bike.

He looked both ways as he crossed the street, tucking his hands into the pocket of his jeans and doing a light jog to clear the street.

He walked up to the house, inhaling before knocking on the door.

Victoria answered the door with a smile on her face. "Hello, Zero."

Cole bowed his head and smiled. "Ma'am. I was waiting…"

"I saw you waiting, I was wondering if I was going to have to kill you, Cole. Next time, just come to the door and make your intentions clear before you sit outside of someone's home for an hour."

Cole gave her a half smile before nodding his head again. "That makes sense. I apologize."

The warm smile that adorned Victoria's face returned. "Come inside, he's in his study."

"Thank you," Cole mumbled as he walking into the older home. He lingered in the living room.

After a moment, Nacobi's father walked into the room, wiping his hands on a napkin before his eyes landed on Cole.

He greeted him with a warm hug and a pat on the back. "How are you son?"

Cole nodded his head. "I'm good. I need to speak to you about something that came up with Nacobi."

Scott Miles frowned at Cole, tilting his head to the side. "What about her?"

"You know what she does?"

Scott consented. "I do. She's a cleaner."

Cole felt himself on the brink of snapping. "You okay with that shit?"

Scott overlooked Cole's anger. "You are in a relationship with Nacobi; you should know that telling her what to do never goes over well."

"Did you have anything to do with this?"

"You and I both know that's not my field of expertise. I honestly don't know how the hell Nacobi became a cleaner. How did you find out?"

"She's my woman, it's my job to know everything about her. So, imagine my surprise when I found surveillance of her dumping a body?"

"Surveillance?"

"Yeah, surveillance."

"Dumping a body?"

Cole grimaced. "Yeah, a got damn body!"

"She's usually extremely careful."

"No one is perfect," Cole snapped. "She got caught slippin', I just thank GOD I was the one who found it. I don't know why she wouldn't tell me this about her."

"That's not something that one would just come out and say."

"I don't give a fuck." Cole shook his head. "I don't even know what to do about this shit. I want her to know that I know, but I want her to be the one to tell me. I want her to be honest."

"Cole, you have to understand that Nacobi is a different type of woman. She's very guarded."

"She has no reason to be, not with me."

"You've hid things from her as well..."

"I did that shit to protect her. You know that. You fucking know that."

"Cole..."

"Everything I've ever done is to protect her. From the minute, you asked me to take that fucking shot! To when you asked me to always protect her! From the moment, you asked me to be there for her. You know I have. You know I've always been in the shadows, protecting her, keeping her safe. This shit threw me! How did I not know?"

"She's good at what she does, Cole!"

"I never interfered with shit! When she was fucking that wack ass nigga that couldn't keep his dick in his pants, I was just there, in the fucking shadows. You wouldn't allow me to kill him!"

"You can't hold on to that, Cole. You killing him would have just made things worse! She was in love with him!"

"I LOVED HER! EVEN THEN! I ALWAYS LOVED HER!"

Cole felt his heart do flips in his chest. The thought of losing Nacobi to anything, bothered him beyond description. For the last five years of his life, he's been there for her. Loving her from a distance. In the shadows. When she began to date Romeo, he wanted to kill him. Asked for clearance to do so, but Scott declined. Stated that it would hurt Nacobi more than help her. When Vince him asked to kill her and Ashura, he was down to do it. Just to end her pain, just to get her away from Romeo because it didn't look like she was ever going to leave. He wanted her away from him, and he knew that her loyalty to people was the thing that kept her there.

Every day, he thanked GOD for clearing his head space. For making him realize that he loved her too deep to ever harm her. His love and obsession with Nacobi had roots that went deeper than anything on the surface. She was a part of him. He couldn't harm her. He never would, no matter how much pain she was in, he had to always love her. Even now.

22

"Truth or Dare?"

Cole quirked a brow at Nacobi as his fingers stilled over the buttons of the remote control. Nacobi was still pissed at him, so he was surprised she was even speaking to him.

Nacobi stood off to the side of him with her arms crossed, waiting for Cole to respond to her. She knew he heard her, even though he had the television up loud as hell. "Cole…"

"I'm not a game player, Nacobi."

"That's all you ever do, what the fuck are you saying?"

Cole dropped his head and ran a frustrated hand down his face. "I'm not doing *this shit* with you again!"

"So, is this what you do, Cole? You lie about shit and don't answer to people when you do it?"

"What the fuck, bruh," Cole mumbled as he stood. He turned to Nacobi with a mug on his face. "You really like this arguing shit, don't you? It's what you fucking used to. Niggas that enjoy lying to you and yelling and shit. I don't operate like that."

"But you did lie, Cole!"

"I hid things that I should have told you, but I never fucking lied to you!"

"So, Truth or Dare?"

Cole shook his head as he tossed the remote onto his couch. "I just told you I'm not doing that bullshit!"

"I'll start," Nacobi spoke in a stern voice, determined to get some answers from him about who the hell he is. "Ask me Truth or Dare!"

"No, Nacobi!"

"Fucking ask me," Nacobi snapped as emotions bubbled inside of her. She swallowed hard before she trained her eyes on him. "Ask me! Just give me the decency of being honest with me for one fucking moment. I make love to you, Cole and I don't even know who the fuck you are. That's not fair to me. You don't know me. That's not fair to you, and I'm tired of hiding, so ask me! We promised to be honest with each other. You promised to tell me everything. You don't keep things from people that you love."

Cole licked his lips and ran his fingers through his beard, stroking his chin a few times before he stuffed his hands into his pocket with a shrug. She wanted his truth; he would give it to her. "Truth or Dare?"

"Truth," Nacobi mumbled.

"It is true that you clean up crime scenes so that people get away with murder?"

"Yes," Nacobi answered with no hesitation. "Truth or Dare?"

Cole was still raving over how easily she let those words roll off her tongue. She was keeping secrets too. Hiding things from him and he was one of the best trackers. He should know everything about her but this was something that she kept from him. So easily kept from him and it was such a big part of her. He was disturbed by her confession but he knew the things he was hiding had the power to ruin them.

"Truth or Dare, Cole?"

Cole's eyes found hers in the partially lit room. "Dare," he uttered with a sly smirk.

"I dare you to tell me the truth!" Nacobi crossed her arms over her chest. "Do you kill people?"

"I do."

"Were you at my parents' house because my father is hiring you to kill someone?"

"No. He wanted information on a previous hit."

"A previous hit on who?"

“I thought this was truth or dare.”

Nacobi inhaled as tears gathered in her eyes. “Did you kill Robert Miles?”

“I don’t remember the names of all of my targets.”

“Cole… please.”

“I can’t give you want you want, Nacobi.”

“You can! You just refuse to! Just tell me! Please?!”

“Anything I say to you in regards to your grandfather’s death would be a lie.”

Nacobi looked up at him with complete disbelief in her eyes. “But you know about it?”

“I know of it. Everyone in Texas knew of it, and at the time that it happened, it was the talk of the city. So yes, I know details.”

“Please don’t bullshit me, Cole. I’ve tried to trust you, tried to be secure in you and know that you would tell me the truth about shit, but in this moment, I know that you are lying.” The pain in her eyes made Cole cringe. “Did… did you kill my grandfather? Please, just…”

“No.”

“Did Anthony?”

"No."

"Do you know the person that killed him?"

Cole remained silent.

"Do you?" Nacobi pressed.

"I know of them."

"Who are they?"

"Hitmen."

"Like Code Zero?"

"Code Zero is no longer in operation."

"But like them."

"Yes."

"Do you know who ordered the hit?"

Cole remained silent.

"Do you know who ordered the hit?"

"I can't tell you that. Who ordered the hit is something that you need to ask your father. I can't give you the answer to that."

"You don't want to help me," Nacobi snapped in Cole's face. "Fine! Fucking fine, Cole! I'll find out my got damn self! Fuck you!"

Cole's eyes ballooned at the fire in her eyes. He reached to grab her before she could get out of arms reach, on alert in case she wanted to swing on him. But she didn't swing on him, in fact she didn't even fight him.

"I need to know what's going on."

"Then I suggest that you speak to your father about what happened to your grandfather, baby. I would tell you everything that I know but it's not my place."

"I plan to speak to him about this shit and I plan to have you there with me when I do."

"Wait… what?"

"We're going to my parents' house tomorrow to talk to them about that happened to my grandfather and I want you there."

"As a supportive boyfriend…"

"As a person that knows something that he won't tell me."

"Nacobi…"

"No! I don't care to talk to you about it anymore! We will talk about it tomorrow."

Cole shook his head. Only Nacobi would be in the wrong, completely in the wrong and somehow find a way to flip things on him.

"Why didn't you tell me you were a cleaner?"

Nacobi shrugged as she walked out of the room. "I don't know. I feel like we enjoy keeping shit from each other in this relationship, so I was just going with the flow of things." Nacobi laughed as she pulled her wine out of the freezer, with Cole following behind her.

"I'm not in the mood to play with you."

Nacobi slammed the freezer and mugged Cole before she slammed her bottle on the cabinet. "I don't give a fuck what you not in the mood for. All you've done this entire relationship is lie to me! You think I care about your feelings behind me leaving something out in my description of myself."

Nacobi popped the top from the wine and began to pour her a glass.

"Nacobi…"

"I'm done talking to you right now, Cole."

Cole bit down on his teeth, seething. "Naco…"

"We really are done talking."

"NO. THE. FUCK. WE NOT."

Nacobi looked over at Cole, setting her drink down with a thump as she advanced on him.

Cole got in her face, causing Nacobi to back down slightly. “You wanna ask me everything under the sun, you wanna fucking accuse me of shit, but you can’t answer my question,” Cole stated with a scowl on his face. “You do this loud, demanding shit. You get in my face, put your fucking fingers in my face. Yell. Scream. Fuck you, Cole! All that but when I ask you one question, all of a sudden you no longer want to talk!”

“I don’t…”

“I’m fucking talking,” Cole snapped causing Nacobi to close her mouth. “The only time I can get you to fucking do what I ask is when I’m yelling or fucking your brains out. I’m tired of that shit! I don’t operate like that! I won’t be raising my voice every time I address you just to get you to listen. You gon’ listen to me because I’m the man in this relationship and I take care of you. You not running shit but your mouth.”

Nacobi lowered her head before she crossed her arms over her chest. She was guilty. She didn’t know why she had to be so damn extra all the time! She sometimes wanted to just have an adult conversation, but she was used to what she was used to. Yelling to communicate was something that she was used to. Something that she was so accustomed to that she didn’t really know how to communicate any other way.

Cole looked down at her, heat in his glare that made Nacobi very aware of him. The man that he was, the one who would allow her so much rope to say and do what she wanted until she was hanging herself. She knew that she was at the point of hanging herself.

"My dick is not what controls you. Nothing controls you, but how you react to me should not have to involve my dick every time!"

The mention of his dick had Nacobi's eyes wandering to the print in his gray sweatpants.

"Stop looking at my dick!"

"Okay!" Nacobi whined as she uncrossed her arms.

"I let you get away with that fly ass mouth too much. I think you forget who the fuck I am! I would hate to have to keep reminding you."

"I… Cole…"

"Were you dumping a body at the Trinity in the surveillance footage I pulled of you?"

Nacobi's head was bowed. Her voice was low, childlike. "Yeah, but..."

"Who was it?"

Nacobi shook her head. "I can't tell you that."

Cole crossed his arms over his chest. "Whose body were you dumping?"

Exhaling, Nacobi released her frustration in a groan. "It was Vince."

"Did you kill him?"

"No, I didn't kill him. I never killed anyone from the scenes that I clean. I'm just a cleaner."

Cole didn't have to ask who killed Vince if Nacobi was telling him that she didn't. He knew it had to be Ashura. Nacobi would never lie to him, she may leave out the truth but she didn't lie to him once he asked her something.

"Why the fuck didn't you tell me what you did. You told me that you owned a cleaning service."

"I do! I own a regular cleaning service, but I also clean crime scenes. I've never lied to you."

"But you just don't tell me what I need to know."

"I'm sorry."

Cole shook his head as he turned to grab his key and helmet off the bar. "I'm out."

Nacobi took big steps to get in front of Cole. "Where are you going?"

“Out. Don’t worry about the tape. I scrapped that shit from every server known to man. No one will ever see it.”

Nacobi became nervous. It had nothing to do with the tape or Vince and everything to do with the man in front of her. “I’m sorry, Cole. I swear. I’ll never clean another scene or hide anything else from you. Don’t leave.”

Cole removed her arm from him as he side stepped her, grabbing his jacket off the chair. “I’ll call you later. I’m going to my spot for a minute. I think we need some space or some shit, Nacobi.”

Tears surfaced, threatening to fall. “Cole. Please don’t.”

Cole walked out the apartment before he didn’t have the strength to leave.

23

It was one thing to deal with someone that never cried, having a moment where they no longer wanted to be strong. They wanted to just have one good cry to get it out of their system and move on. It was an entirely different thing to have someone who never cried, have a complete breakdown.

Nacobi wiped her face as she laid on Ashura's lap. This was the position she'd been in for at least the last week. She hadn't spoken to Cole, and he hadn't made any attempts to reach out to her. That bothered her. It shattered her. It was horrible.

"You want to try and call him again?"

Ashura ran her hands through Nacobi's hair, feeling her friend's pain and wanting to do something to help ease it, but knowing that nothing she did or said would make the situation better. She felt partially responsible after hearing why Cole had asked Nacobi for space. She was cleaning a scene for her, and had somehow ended up on that recording.

"He was so pissed when he left. I should have just told him. I should have been honest, now I'm fucked."

“Don’t say that, Nacobi. Cole loves you. He will eventually forgive you.”

“What if *eventually* never comes, and I have to deal with not having him?”

“That won’t happen!”

“You don’t know that. You didn’t see the look in his eyes when he left, Shu-Shu. I begged him not to leave, and he did anyway. It’s like what the fuck, niggas don’t make me beg. Then I beg and you still leave?! It’s like, for real? You for real? It’s like… I’m Nano nigga!”

Ashura frowned to keep from smiling. “Just calm down.”

“No,” Nacobi snapped as she jumped out of Ashura’s lap. “I fuck with me heavy. Cole got me fucked up! This ain’t me! I don’t cry over dudes. I just replace dick! I! Don’t! Chase! Dick!”

“Maybe because you’re in love with him.”

“No bitch! I was in love with Romeo…”

“You weren’t,” Ashura let out with a shake of her head. “You may have thought you loved Romeo. Maybe he made you cry and grabbed emotions out of you, but it was solely because you were giving him your all. You loved him, but you were not in love with him. Of all the times Romeo cheated on you, I’ve never had to hold you while you cried over him. You are in love with Cole.”

Nacobi looked at her best friend, her eyes red from crying, her hair disheveled and out of place, but she was still beautiful. Just a little broken, slightly lost but still beautiful."

"It's about more than his dick, sis," Ashura stated with a shrug.

Nacobi wanted to stay upset but she laughed in spite of herself. "Sometimes I can't stand you," Nacobi mumbled as she crawled back onto Ashura's lap, grabbing her hand, and placing it back in her head so that she could massage it. "I need to get my metahuman back."

"Bitch," Ashura spat before she cracked up laughing. "You did not just call him a metahuman."

"His dick is abnormally big, and his head game is…"

"I don't careeeeee," Ashura yelled as she snatched her hands out of Nacobi's hair and covered her ears. "I cannot tell you how much I don't care!"

"But, it's the reason why I'm like this."

"It's not."

"What other reason would I be this fucked up, Shu- Shu?"

"I just told you, it's because you love him."

"I do love him," Nacobi mumbled.

"Wait... what?" Though Nacobi had confessed her love to Cole, she never told Ashura that she had done so. It was something that she was still attempting to decipher herself.

Nacobi held her head down. "I didn't tell you because I was scared that something like this would happen. That love would blow up in my face. I feel like I ruin everything when it comes to my relationships. You the only somebody that seems to stick around."

"It's because your ass is fat," Ashura joked with her tongue out.

"Shut up!" Nacobi cast her eyes to the ground, a foreign sense of vulnerability taking over her. "I lost him."

Ashura stood and grabbed her friend. "Trust me, you didn't lose him. If I've learned anything since meeting Cole, it's that he cares about you deeply. There is no way that you lost him. But, I know a way to determine how close you are to getting him back."

Nacobi frowned. "How when he not even talking to me?"

Ashura gave Nacobi a sneaky smile. "I might get in trouble for this but...get dressed."

***

Nacobi was in shock. "Bitch, this is your plan?"

Ashura pulled her dress down before she whirled around with her drink in her hand, dancing wildly in the middle of the crowded club. Nacobi looked around to see if she could see Cole, but as she expected, he wasn't there.

"Why would you think this would get him to talk to me?"

Ashura was dancing so hard, she barely heard Nacobi. "What?"

"Bitch," Nacobi mussed. "I don't know why I listened to you. I wanna go back to the house."

"Give it more time, Nacobi." Ashura laughed as she danced. "He won't come out of hiding if you just standing there. Dance bitch."

Nacobi looked at Ashura like she was crazy. "What a difference some black dick makes," she mumbled as she began to move.

She felt stupid because she was all the way off beat. She would admit that she looked good; her dress hugged her hips and her hair was done in huge wand curls that fell around her face and shoulders. She sipped from her drink and rolled her eyes as she began to dance, getting on beat with Ashura, who was surprising the hell out of her. If Anthony was here, he'd have her ass snatched up by now. That was another reason she knew Cole was nowhere near her. Her heart was heavy, but she danced, trying to enjoy her friend, who seemed to be having the time of her life.

Nacobi felt a presence behind her, but she knew it was the man she wanted because her heart didn't race, the hair on her body didn't stand on end. Her eyes were already rolling in her head when he grabbed her.

"Say shawty…"

"I'm not interested," Nacobi spoke loud enough for the guy to hear over the music.

"You don't even know what I want yet."

Nacobi turned around slowly. "I don't care what you…"

"Dance with him," Ashura spoke in her ear. "Throw that ass in a circle on him."

Nacobi turned to Ashura. "What?"

"Just do it!"

Nacobi was still trying to determine what the hell had gotten into Ashura when she felt old boy press against her. "Listen to your friend and dance with me."

Nacobi shook her head as she turned her back to ol boy. She was about to walk off the dance floor, realizing that this was a dummy mission, until she felt *him*.

His presence almost knocked the wind out of her and she hadn't laid eyes on him yet. She felt him touch her but she didn't see him.

His ability to be ubiquity to her, made her swoon. She inhaled, flowing with the air into her lungs was his scent. It was all over her at once. Too much.

Nacobi began to move, closing her eyes, and feeling him all over her and wanting to be close to him but not knowing exactly how to do that and stand in place. She bent over, bouncing her ass on the stranger behind her while he gripped her waist. She stood, then grinded her hips against him until she was wrapped in his arms. The song changed to one of a slower tempo, and Nacobi immediately followed the flow of the DJ. Her drink slipped from her hands, she felt intoxicated but it wasn't from the watered-down ass drink she consumed. It was *him*.

Nacobi opened her eyes when the presence of the man behind her seemingly vanished. She looked around and noticed that Ashura was no longer on the dance floor with her neither.

"What the fu…"

Her words were halted by the force of her arm being pulled. She struggled to keep up with the speed of Cole as he pushed people out of the way, successfully pulling her off the dancefloor and into a quiet corner. Then… she was face to face with *him*.

His eyes were dark marbles, focused on her face. His chest rose and feel with pending frustration and his hands clenched then relaxed with each breath he took. He closed his eyes, trying to calm his racing heart before he slammed a hand against the wall beside Nacobi's head, causing her to release a squeal.

"You like fuckin' with me, Nano. That's it! Tell me! TELL ME!"

"Cole, I just…"

"Why the fuck is you out here?! Why are you here?!"

Nacobi swallowed. "I wanted to get out the house and…"

"You want to be the reason somebody gets killed in this bitch? That it!"

Nacobi shook her head. This wasn't Cole. Cole didn't speak like this. Cole never raised his voice. This person was different, and Nacobi was woman enough to admit… she was terrified.

"Calm down, please."

Cole stared hard at her. "You like fucking with me."

"I just wanted you to talk to me. I was just trying to…"

"Leave here, Nacobi. Leave now. If you don't, I won't have shit else to say to you ever. Get the fuck out of this club!"

With that, Cole walked down the hallway to the emergency exit, setting the siren off as if it were normal.

"Cole!"

He didn't respond to her, he kept walking as if she didn't mean anything to him. Nacobi released a breath that she wasn't aware she was holding as she tightened her grip on the clutch she carried. Her mind raced with a million thoughts as she stood against the wall, fighting back tears.

Ashura seemed to appear out of nowhere, at her side, like always. "You okay?"

Nacobi nodded her head, unable to speak. She kept nodding until her nod turned into a shake and tears escaped her eyes. She covered her face with her hands as she began to sob. Ashura held her. "It's okay. He's just pissed, Nacobi. It will be okay."

24

Like she expected, Ashura was in deep water over the stunt she pulled with Nacobi. Before Cole snapped on her, Ashura was being snatched and pulled off the dance floor. Anthony allowed her time to go and get Nacobi once Cole left, but after that, he took her to her house to grab some more things, then she was forced to come to his place. His place was different from hers in the sense that it was smaller, but it felt more like home than her house ever did.

Ashura hadn't heard Anthony come into the house but, he was watching her. Closely.

"Ashura?"

Ashura backed away from Anthony, not sure of what she wanted to say to him. His demeanor made her skin tingle on end. The aura that his presence cast through the room was nothing short of unnerving.

"What is that in your hand, Ashura?"

His voice didn't shift in its octave. His face did nothing to give away his mood. He was...void of anything.

"Nothing," Ashura squeaked. She cleared her throat before her eyes danced back to his. "Nothing, Anthony."

In his close assessment of her, Anthony could detect a number of things. One, radiating off her as if it was becoming of her— she was scared. Scared... not in the sense that she felt she was in danger. No. Scared nervous was what he felt. He decided against moving from his position across the room, not yet anyway. "Tell me what you have."

"I don't..."

"Don't lie to me. That shit just gon' piss me off, and I don't feel like being in that headspace, so be honest."

Ashura swallowed, making a solid attempt at clearing the dryness that her throat felt. "Anthony..."

"You wanna hide shit from me as if I don't know you inside and out." Anthony took a step before he released a sexy chuckle, grabbing the box that Ashura clearly forgot to discard off the dresser. "You wanna be fucked or made love to because a nigga like me... I can deliver either or."

Ashura closed her eyes, forcing her heart rate to slow before she looked back up at Anthony. "I didn't think you were coming back tonight."

Anthony nodded, he gathered that much. "Had some shit to tend to, now I'm back. The fact that you're here is reason enough to come home."

Ashura ran her free hand down the front of her gown before she nervously tucked her lip between her teeth. "So, what are your plans for the rest of the night?"

Anthony's eyebrows lowered in confusion. "What the fuck you mean? You tryna kick me out my own spot?"

Ashura recovered quickly. "I would never kick you out, Anthony. I actually missed you and was waiting for you to come back."

Anthony pointed to the object that Ashura was failing terribly at hiding. "So," he stepped closer, coming to a stop inches away from her. He pulled her hand that held her "rabbit" from behind her back. Taking it from her hand, his eyes found hers, "You decided to play in my pussy?"

Ashura lowered her head in complete embarrassment. "How did you even get in here?"

Anthony dropped Ashura's toy and pulled both her hands in front of him, looking into her eyes as he placed her fingers to his mouth. "Did you use these too or just that other shit?"

Ashura refused to answer that question.

"Are you pissed that you were caught or that you were interrupted?"

Again, Ashura remained quiet.

Anthony looked into her eyes as he stuck his tongue out to slide across the tips of her fingers. He closed his eyes, releasing a groan as the taste of her took over his taste buds. "Of course, you used them."

Ashura tried to pull her hand away, but he grabbed her, wrapping one arm around her and using the other to push her robe off her shoulder. "You wanna cum, Ashura?"

Labored breaths were the only thing Ashura could manage that would partially translate as a response.

Once she was naked, Ashura found herself being lifted into Anthony's arms as he moved to spread her out on her bed. Looking up at Anthony, she couldn't gauge what he was thinking. Self-pleasure was something that she had to do ritually while she was with Vince, but she had a strong feeling Anthony didn't like the idea of her pleasing herself very much.

"Don't do that shit, Ashura," he scolded as he removed his clothes. When he was naked, he reached for her, his fingers dwelling inside the wetness between her legs, causing her lids to flutter. "You wanna cum... you call Daddy."

Ashura closed her eyes as his tongue found her center. Getting up on her elbows, she watched his tongue slide between her folds, torturously slow, until it hit her clit, causing her thighs to shake at its contact. She was sensitive for a number of reasons.

Her head fell back as a small cry traveled beyond her lips from deep within her. She felt everything his tongue did. Every angle it hit and the moment he incorporated his fingers, sliding two of them into her at the same pace as his tongue and her clit, touched each other.

She was cumin'... too soon.

"Ugh!" A cry ripped from her lips as her body folded toward his. She tried to push his head away but he was latched onto her as if this would be his last meal as a free man. "Anthony! Fuck!"

Selfish. She was being selfish and so was he. Not caring that she came already, Anthony kept his tongue pushed against her and his fingers planted inside of her until she was cumin again.

Too spent to fight him off, Ashura just allowed her orgasm to have its way. Her mouth went slack as her entire body tensed them relaxed in a way that had her falling back onto the bed.

"You so fucking good at that," Ashura confessed in her drunken state. "So damn good."

Anthony moved up her, rubbing her juices from his lips, leaving remnants of her in his beard. He grabbed her legs and pushed them back, rubbing his dick inside her wetness before he slapped the head of it against her clit, causing her to flinch.

Slowly, he began to feed her dick. Ashura eyes stayed on Anthony until the depth he hit became too much. She placed her hand on his stomach but he quickly slapped it away before going deeper.

"Anth..."

"I don't wanna hear that shit!"

"It's too much!"

"Handle that shit anyway. Be a big girl!" Anthony shifted deeper, causing Ashura to cry out. "Be nasty for Daddy!"

Anthony slammed into at the rate of a piston. His hips rotating at angles that had Ashura clawing at his back.

"Oh shit, Anthony!"

"Damnnnn, Shu-Shu."

Ashura felt the muscles in her stomach flex and knew she was cumin again. The pressure was far too much.

"Fuck me! Please don't stop!"

Anthony got on his knees, pushing Ashura legs back further as he looked at her, never losing his tempo. "My dick feel better than that shit you had?"

Ashura nodded her head rapidly as her orgasm backpacked up her spin.

"I need to hear that shit, Shu-Shu!"

"It does!"

"What you talking 'bout," Anthony asked as his finger moved up to caress her breast.

Ashura screamed from her gut as her legs shook on their own accord, this orgasm far stronger than the other.

"Cum for daddy," Anthony mumbled under her, more for him than for her. "Tell me I'm better!"

"You better!"

"The best?"

Ashura grabbed the sheets of the bed to prevent harm to Anthony. "You the mothafuckin G.O.A.T.!"

25

Nacobi sat in her parents living room with a look of complete confusion on her face.

"Run that back to me."

Her father stole a glance at her mother before he turned to look back at Nacobi. "I wanted to be honest with you. I wanted to tell you everything about what happened to your grandfather. but there are just some things that I don't want you involved in."

"What the hell? Daddy, how do you know Cole?"

"Both Cole and Anthony were a part of Operation Union. You remember that?"

Nacobi nodded her head. "I thought you didn't get clearance on that. I thought that you couldn't get it done."

Scott nodded his head. "We did it under the table. There were about five men that volunteered; Cole and Anthony also known as Code Zero, were two of them.

Nacobi held her head in her hands to ease the tension gathering at her temples. "So, wait Daddy. You created Code Zero?"

"As well as Stone and two others. The only three that I am still in contact with are Code Zero and Stone. The other two are dead.

Nacobi shook her head in confusion. "Daddy…"

"Cole has been in your life for the last five years, Nacobi. He has been protecting you, he has been keeping you safe. Cole is in love with you, has been in love with you for a very long time. He was confused about how he felt about you, didn't know how to express it or what was happening to him but he does. He loves you."

Nacobi felt like a fool. She had accused Cole of the worst shit but he was the exact opposite of that. He was there to protect her. Like he said he was when she first accused him of foul play. "I keep messing this up."

Nacobi's mother reached out and touched her hand. "Give him time."

"Why would you keep this from me, Daddy? Why wouldn't you tell me this? Ma, you straight up lied to me. You told me that you didn't know Cole."

"At the time, I couldn't tell you that I knew him. I wanted that to be something that you talked to your father and Cole about. That was the only reason I didn't tell you. I understand why you would be upset."

"Why has he been in my life? Why did I need a bodyguard?"

Scott wrung his hands together. “Right after the Operation Union, I got threats on all of our lives. I couldn’t chance anything happening to you, and I knew that I couldn’t tell you without you freaking out, so I just placed Zero in your life to keep you safe. Your grandfather ditched his detail to go to take a trip to a casino, the other two men that I created, Snake and Rambo were paid to betray me and kill him.” Scott swallowed the lump in his throat as tears gathered in Nacobi’s eyes. Scott had dealt with his father's death and the part he played in it a long time ago, but he knew his daughter wouldn’t be able to handle this reveal as he did. “Sweetheart, I didn’t tell you because…”

“Because it's your fault,” Nacobi choked out. “It's your fault!”

“It was my fault,” Scott concluded. “If I could change things then I would, but there is no way for me to do that, Nacobi.”

“Why didn’t you tell me this? I’ve been trying to figure it out. Oh, my God, I accused Cole!”

“I'm sorry! I didn’t tell you because I wanted to keep you safe!”

“This is not something that you keep from me, Daddy! This is…”

“Nacobi,” her mother coached, “try to understand.”

“This is bullshit! I can't believe you lied to me,” she spat at her mother. “And you,” she directed at her father. “Like real shit, both of y’all can kiss my ass!”

Crowned 2: The Return of a Savage

Nacobi walked out of her parent's home, far more confused that what she was when she came.

26

Ashura pulled her face out of the trash can to catch her breath before she was hurling in the trash can again. Her body heaved once it was empty, her head was spinning and she was having a hard time pulling herself together.

She felt too weak to move, but she somehow made it to the sink to wash her face and brush her teeth before crawling back into her bed.

She pulled the covers up and over her body before grabbing her duvet and pulling it over her as well. She exhaled as her body settled, thanking GOD for the settling of her stomach. She hated being sick, but she knew this wasn't just a common cold. Her cycle was nonexistent, and she knew she was pregnant. She knew her body well enough to know that something was off with her and she knew that thing was her being pregnant.

She needed to speak with Anthony. She was scared. She didn't want a repeat of the last time she was pregnant. She didn't even know if she could carry a baby full term. She was terrified of losing this baby because whether or not she was ready, she wanted a baby. A healthy baby.

Sometime after she crawled back into the bed, she must've fallen asleep because she was awakened by Anthony's weight dipping the bed in front of her.

Her eyes came open slowly as Anthony sat a bag down on the dresser then leaned back on the bed, he reached out to push her hair out of her face before he leaned down and kissed her forehead.

"You still don't feel good?"

Ashura shook her head. "I think I may need to…"

Anthony sat a box down in front of her before he stood. "I'm about to go make you some soup and tea. You take that and by the time it's ready, I'll be back in here."

Anthony went to leave out of the room.

"Wait," Ashura whispered harshly. "What… can I ask you something?"

"If it's about to be some dumb shit then don't even ask me."

Ashura dropped her head. "Please, Anthony."

Anthony crossed his arms over his chest as he looked at her. "What is it?"

Ashura licked her lips nervously before her eyes connected with his. "What if I am pregnant? What… what would you want me to do?"

"That would be the stupid shit I was referring to."

"I just want…"

"I would never allow you to kill my fucking seed, Ashura."

Immediately, Ashura nodded her head. "No, I know that. I just. I don't know. I just… I've been pregnant before and I lost it. I just… don't want you to be disappointed if I can't…"

"What happened the first time that you were pregnant?"

Ashura dropped her head and Anthony moved to sit in back on the bed in front of her. Ashura looked up at him, her eyes glazed over. "I carried her full term. I got checkups, I took my vitamins and pills, I didn't miss an appointment. I was about eight months when Vince came in drunk one night. He um… pushed me down the stairs and I started bleeding. I had to steal the car keys and drive myself to the hospital. By the time I made it, she was gone. She didn't make it."

Anthony grabbed her and pulled her into his arms before she could break down but as soon as she was in his arms, the bough broke. Her wrapped her arms around Anthony as her soft cries turned into sobs. Again, very similar to last time, he just held her, stroking her hair, rocking her and whispering in her ear that everything would be okay. She wasn't sure. She didn't feel like everything would be okay. She felt like her life, her happiness was about to be taken on a worldwide extravaganza, yet again.

"I would never do anything to hurt you, Ashura."

"I know that, Anthony. I would never question that."

"So, if you are pregnant, you should know that I plan to take care of you and our baby. Don't say shit about my age; don't say shit about your past or mine. We would be parents and we would take care of our baby together. Together. So, if you had any doubt in your head that I wasn't here for the long haul, then you should know that shit by now."

Ashura leaned down and kissed him. "I don't care about your age. I don't care about how we met. I only care about the way my heart responds to your presence. The way love races to greet you at my lips every time you lean in to kiss me. You, Anthony Drake, are the man that I love, and crave, and need. I want you to always know that."

Anthony smiled up at her. "I do know that. So, get to taking this test, and I'll go get you some soup ready."

Ashura consented as she climbed out of his lap and back out of bed to take the test. She smiled and did a giddy dance before she opened the box and took the test, after a minute of running water.

She didn't need this test to tell her she was pregnant. She knew she was, it was just a matter of how far along she was. But the test confirmed her suspicions, she was indeed pregnant. She washed her hands and came out of the bathroom, ten minutes later with the test in her hand. Anthony was entering the room at the same time with a bowl of steaming soup and a cup of tea. He set the tray down on the nightstand and looked over at her.

"What that shit say?"

Ashura smiled at him. "It says that you're going to be a daddy."

Anthony's eyes ballooned before they settled back into their normal state. "What the fuck?!" he exclaimed, causing Ashura to frown.

"You just said…"

"I wonder when I got yo ass pregnant. Prolly in Fiji, huh? I was swimming in that shit the whole trip!" Anthony shook his head with a huge smile on his face. "I can't believe you pregnant."

Ashura stood, perplexed. "So, are you happy or sad?!"

Anthony laughed as he walked up to her, wrapping her in his arms and placing kisses all over her face. Ashura smiled as he suspended her up in the air. "Why you ask me that shit, Ashura? I'm happy as fuck. I love you and you about to have my baby. Shit is perfect."

Ashura smiled at him before she kissed him.

"I don't know the first thing about being a father, but I promise not to let you down. You or our baby."

Ashura felt emotions swell inside of her as her feet touched the ground. “I don’t have a doubt in my mind that you’ll be amazing.”

Uncertainty flashed in Anthony’s eyes, momentarily before joy returned. “I will. I won’t fail. I won’t fail you.”

Ashura leaned back and kissed Anthony, running her thumbs over his eyebrows and lips. “I won’t let you fail.”

***

27

Cole lifted the weight above his head, vigorously attempting to rid himself of thoughts of Nacobi. Seeing her at the club only made how need for her stronger and that was the last thing he wanted.

It seemed to him that the only thing he and Nacobi could get right is fucking each other, Outside of that, everything was a lie. A lie that they convinced themselves needed to be told in order for the other to be content. But that wasn't the case, not with him. The thing he was withholding from her was Danielle. That was a part of his past, one that he recently discovered would have no impact on the future that he would share with Nacobi. Like he figured, Danielle's child wasn't his. He knew that from jump, but he wanted to be sure, and the only way that he could do that was to get a test. Now that he knew what happened between them would have no bearing on him and Nacobi, he was ready to move forward with her. But, in digging into the "cleaning service" Nacobi used as a cover up, he discovered more about her. Things that she should have shared with him, being that he was so honest and open with her.

This sounded like he was overreacting. Sounded as if he wasn't fair to her. Sounded like his ego was wounded, and maybe all of those things were factors in the way he was acting, but they weren't the main reason. Nacobi hid something from him that could have caused him to lose her.

The fucking thought of not having her was enough to push him over the edge.

He loved her.

Loved her.

Deep. Current. Forever.

She was his.

His only.

For- fucking- ever!

"And the day after that shit," he grunted as he lifted the weight over his head.

He placed the weights on the bench before he stood and grabbed a towel off the rack. He walked into his bathroom so that he could shower, pausing when his phone vibrated on the nightstand beside his bed.

He knew who it was. He could feel it.

He almost tripped over himself attempting to get to the phone. He grabbed it, sliding his thumb across it, but he didn't speak.

"Hello," Nacobi spoke on the other end. "Cole…"

"What is it?"

Nacobi exhaled. "Why are you doing this? I said that I was sorry. I want to fix this. I spoke to my parents…I know…I know that you didn't have anything to do with my grandfather's death, and I know that you've been in my life for a long time. I'm… Cole, I'm confused and I'm lost and I feel like I can't trust anyone. I'm sorry for the way that I talked to you. I'm sorry for not telling you what I did."

"You don't understand the severity of leaving me out of the loop of what you actually do."

"I fucked up. I talked to my parents, Cole. I know everything. I shouldn't have assumed and I should have told you about what I did for a living. I messed up and I can admit that. I'm sorry."

Her voice and the emptiness that it held almost broke him. Nacobi was used to a different type of man, one that was not him. "You don't understand, Nacobi."

"I won't do it anymore, Cole."

"You damn right you won't. That's not my issue, that shit is a no brainer. You won't be doing that or any of that other stupid shit you were doing."

"Okay, so what are we doing?"

Cole stood still, his eyes wide in the dark room. "What do you mean?"

"How long do you plan to be on this bullshit? How long do you expect me to wait until you're over it?"

"Until I'm ready!"

"Until you're ready?"

"Yeah!"

Nacobi sucked her teeth as she nodded her head, her stubbornness not allowing her to fold to Cole. "Okay, I see now you on that bullshit and I tried to be patient while you went through whatever the fuck it is you're going through but now I'm done. Fuck you, Cole!"

Cole chuckled. "Is this the way you call and makeup with someone when you're in the wrong, Nacobi? If so, you don't really apologize well."

"Fuck you and yo nerdy ass ways, and yo *I don't like when you curse ass!* I don't care, Cole. I don't!"

"You like cursing, you like being loud and annoying. You can have that shit, Nacobi!"

"Yeah, I do like that shit, so fuck you, nigga!"

"Fuck me," Cole spat with venom. "Fuck you!"

"No fuck you nigga!" Nacobi snapped. "Fuck you! I don't have to chase you! We gon' be like this until you ready? Fuck you think this is, Burger King? You can't have it your way!"

"No, you can't have it your way, Nacobi. That's the problem! You dead wrong but flipping out on me!"

"I don't need you! You can suck my dick!"

"Nah," Cole stated with a slur. "You can suck mine though!"

"I ain't putting my mouth near that shit ever again, but I'll bless another nigga with this head game. Fuckkk you!"

Cole felt his blood boil. "Don't fuck with me."

"Tell that to the next bitch! I bet she won't fuck you like me. Nigga no one gets as wet as Nano! But like I said, on to the next! Or maybe I'll go fuck with my old nigga. It doesn't matter! You don't matter!"

"You ain't stupid, Nacobi."

"You gon' let all this good shit go to waste over some bullshit? So… let's see who else fucking with me like I fuck with my damn self! Kiss my ass!"

"You and that nigga will get bodied on sight. That's some shit you want?"

"You ain't gon' do shit!"

"Try it and see, sweetheart. You should know by now that I don't talk about the shit I plan to do. I been about that action so, try me."

"Why does it even matter to you?"

Cole shook his head. "That's your issue, Nacobi. You want things on your time, you want to control things but I keep telling you that I am not the man to allow you to do that. You want me to hop when you tell me to, and that shit ain't happening. But trust me when I tell you, if I find out you fucking around, it won't be cute."

***

Never having a reason to love or live was depressing. The one thing that gave him meaning beyond what he could ever imagine, just walked in wearing the sexiest dress he'd ever seen on a woman. She had her breast pushed up, ass on display looking like a video vixen that was far too classy to ever showcase her assets in a music video. The perfect contradiction.

She knew he was a tracker.

Knew he had no issues finding people, their whereabouts as well as whom they were with at the time. She knew all of this and still, she seemed to want to press him. Then to see her, smiling in the face of another man as if she weren't his. As if he hadn't made love to her so many times that he lost count. As if they hadn't expressed the love that they have for each other. As if he hadn't warned her a day ago, that this type of activity would end in someone getting hurt. She didn’t believe him. That just pissed him off more than he was already enraged.

His entire life, Cole has dealt with insecurity. Seeing the woman, he loved beyond understanding flirt with someone else had him feeling invalid. It took him back to high school, where he first made an attempt at dating, only to be made a fool of. He promised that he would never ever place himself in the position to feel that way again. But in spite of that, he fell in love with Nacobi Miles.

Cole took large steps as he gained ground on Nacobi and her *date*, she wasn't even aware he'd spotted her. She went to laugh at something that was said to her when she was snatched out of her seat by her arm.

She almost stumbled in her heels before she gained her balance, ready to defend herself before Cole’s eyes connected with hers.

Cole got in her face. "You don't know who the fuck you playing with, Nacobi. I'll kill this man in front of all these people and not think twice about it. I don't give a fuck! I know you feeling yourself and you got niggas wanting you left and right, but this ain't going down!"

"Say nigga! Who the fuck..."

Romeo's words got caught in his throat as he came face to face with Cole's Desert Eagle.

"Cole, calm down, please," Nacobi pleaded in a soft voice. "It's not what it looks like."

Cole didn't release his grip on Nacobi nor move his gun out the face of Romeo. "You like this shit, don't you?"

"I don't…"

"You like testing me. Seeing what I'm gone do, seeing if I'm really about the shit I talk about. You wanna make me tick, Nacobi?"

"No, baby," Nacobi pleaded as Cole used his thumb to click the safety off the gun. "Cole, you can't do this."

"Why the fuck would you place me in the position to have to? Why are you out here with this nigga?"

Nacobi nodded and swallowed. "You're right! Let's just go!"

Cole squinted as recognition hit him. "This is your ex."

Nacobi became terrified. "Cole...please."

Romeo for whatever reason saw his life flash before his eyes. "Look man, I don't know what she told you but…"

"She ain't told me shit! I don't know why you're in her presence!"

"She... she just called me and…"

Cole was in a trance, tunnel vision and white noise. He saw his lips moving, pleading for his life but his heart turned cold the moment he saw him making Nacobi smile. He was the only man that was supposed to be doing that shit. No one else! The only thing that was in his scope was Romeo. His finger itched to press the trigger; he wasn't sure what was holding him back.

"You just jump when good pussy calls you?"

The question was rhetorical; he wished Romeo would answer that shit. It would give him the clearance he needed to end his life.

"I don't want no trouble, bruh… I just came because she called me."

"Cole, let's just leave. They're going to call the police. You're scaring people."

Cole looked back at Nacobi with acrimonious eyes, he could feel himself getting more deranged by the moment. He looked over at Romeo, who hadn't moved a muscle since their encounter. "My nigga, I don't want you near her. Act like she got a fucking two state restraining order against you. If I catch you in the same zip code as her, you die. That's it. You got me?!"

Romeo nodded his head rapidly, "I got you. I got you!"

"Fuck outta here," Cole spat as he dropped his arm, tucking his gun back into its place.

Romeo kept his hands up, back peddling to get away from Cole before he could change his mind. Fear raced through his body until he made it to his car.

Nacobi released a deep sigh as she turned to move away from Cole, but he held on to her.

“I can’t believe you just did that!”

“But I did,” Cole spat. “You better be glad I didn’t do more. Why they fuck are you out with this nigga? What the fuck is wrong with you?”

Nacobi snatched from him. “Don’t worry about it, Cole! You don’t want me, right? Why are you here? You the mothafucka that’s out of place! But you can stay because I’m leaving!”

Cole released her, allowing her to leave, knowing that he would never allow her to get too far. “You heard what I told ol dude, Nacobi. Same shit applies to you.”

28

Ashura kept stealing glances at Nacobi as she sat to the left of her, eating ice cream and grunting every so often. After revealing to Ashura that her father was the man responsible for Code Zero, as well as the fact that Cole had been in her life as her protector for the last two years, it was clear she had a lot on her mind. Ashura wondered if now would be a good time to let her in on the fact that she was going to be a GOD mother soon.

Ashura and Nacobi hadn't seen each other much at all lately; between Ashura being up under Anthony twenty-four seven and Nacobi doing everything in her power to dodge Cole, they only talked on the phone. It seemed like they were worlds apart, even though they were sitting in the same room.

"Cole pulled a gun on Romeo."

Ashura looked at her friend for clarity. "What?"

"I went out with Romeo…"

"Why the fuck would you do that?"

"I don't know," Nacobi spat. "I wanted to go out with him. It wasn't shit. We just went to dinner."

"You don't just go to dinner with your ex."

"Damnnn," Nacobi groaned as she stood and faced Ashura, who was still sitting on the couch with her legs tucked under her. "Can you not judge me? I'm so tired of everyone…"

"Calm down," Ashura stated, placing her hand on the couch and pushing up off of it so that she could stand. "I'm not judging you."

"Well, it sounds like you are."

"But I'm not."

Nacobi crossed her arms over chest and rolled her eyes. "I don't care for Romeo, and that's my cousin. I told you from the beginning not to get involved with his ass. You didn't listen. Romeo could never love you on the same level that Cole loves you. Period. He's too selfish. You deserve better."

"I'm not fucking him, Ashura."

"But when you stay in the presence of a fuck boy for too long, his aura starts to rub off on you."

Nacobi frowned as she shook her head. "I don't know what's gotten into you, but I'm not sure if I'm fucking with it!"

"What so ever do you mean," Ashura teased. "I've always been honest with you. I've always kept it real with you. That's what we do. I call you out on your shit, and you call me out on mine. That's what we are to each other. This right here, what you are doing with Cole, is bullshit."

"How about the way that Cole is treating me is bullshit!"

Ashura shrugged. "I can't say that I blame him for feeling the way that he does. You kept something big from him…"

"Let's not forget who the fuck I was dumping, Ashura. Let's not forget who I did that for. I did that for you!"

"I know who you were dumping. I owe a lot to you, Nacobi. You won't catch me saying otherwise, but you should always have open communication in your relationship. Especially with a man like Cole, he wants to protect you!"

"I don't need protection!"

"Clearly you do! If it weren't for him erasing the video, you would have had something pending against you that could put you in jail for the rest of your life."

"That's the risk that I take," Nacobi snapped. "I don't have shit to live for! I never have! I know the line of business I'm in. Unlike you, I didn't run from my future; I embraced that shit. It owned who I am a long time ago!"

"Who are you exactly, Nacobi?"

"Nacobi Miles, cleaner, friend…"

"GOD mother," Ashura interrupted to say.

Nacobi's expression went from anger to disoriented. "What?"

"Go ahead," Ashura pressed. "Continue your spiel!"

"No... what do you mean GOD mother?"

Ashura gave Nacobi a weak smile. "I'm pregnant."

"What the hell you mean you pregnant?"

Ashura chuckled. "Just what I said… I'm pregnant!"

Nacobi couldn't contain her smile. "Anthony got cho ass?!"

Ashura's smile deepened. "Yeah. I took a few test last week, and they were all positive so, I made an appointment for next week.

Nacobi sat down, feeling like the weight of the world was just placed in her lap. Like she was a loose nigga, going around fucking everyone and one of his thots just dropped an "I'm late" bomb on him. She felt as if she just found out she were the one pregnant and not Ashura.

"So, you pregnant? When were you going to tell me?"

"We haven't been exactly talking, Nacobi."

Nacobi huffed and tossed her hair over her shoulder. "This ain't something you just spring on a nigga, man. I need time to prepare. I ain't ready to be no GOD momma!"

Ashura tucked her lip in so that she wouldn't laugh because the look on Nacobi's face was so serious. "You have to get ready because GOD willing, it's happening.

"Are you sure? How many test did you take? Like them shits one hundred percent, though?"

"Yes, Nacobi."

Nacobi huffed again, running a stressed hand down her face. "Niggas don't believe in condoms no more or some shit? What the hell I'm supposed to do with a GOD baby?"

"Y'all can go to the mall and dress alike, give me breaks when I need them. Love him or her and stay out of jail so that you can be a part of their life."

A knock at the door had both of them standing at attention. Nacobi looked at Ashura with a mug on her face. "Go to the back."

"No," Ashura declined.

"I am not debating with you! Take yo butt to the back until I tell you it's clear!"

"Please don't start acting like I'm handicapped!"

"You not about to put my GOD baby in danger! Carry yo stubborn tail to the back. It's more than likely just ya baby daddy anyway."

Ashura threw her hands up as she walked into the back room, shaking her head. She didn't think Nacobi knew how much she sounded like a man.

Nacobi waited until Ashura was out of sight before she pulled the gun from her back. She walked to the door slowly, carefully peeking through the peephole before her entire body completely tensed.

Cole Remington.

He stood on the other side of the door, his signature all black attire, shades on his face, thick pink lips on display.

Nacobi felt her traitorous body respond to him, even though they had a door separating them. She expired a breath before she turned, placing her back to the door.

"I know you're there, Nacobi."

Nacobi rolled her eyes in her head. "Why are you here?"

Cole placed his forehead on the door, his body drained and his life in disarray. His hand slid up the door as if it were her, as if she were the one thing he was touching. His voice was low, croaked when he stated, "I need you, Baby."

"Cole, we keep doing this back and forth shit. I'm getting whiplash."

Cole gritted his teeth. "You hid things!"

"We both did, Cole. You hid things too! We both are guilty of the same thing but somehow you feel entitled to feel a way."

Cole pressed his forehead to the door. "Open."

"No, Cole."

"Please? I miss you! Please, come with me. I just need to be able to touch you. I just…wanna taste my Nano."

"Now how the hell am I supposed to be able to say no to that shit", whined as she turned her back to the door and slid down it. She ran her fingers through her hair before she stood again. She turned to face the door, all the strength she had left in her present as she spoke, "No, Cole!"

"You can ride my face."

Nacobi grabbed the door handle and pulled it open. "I just uh…imma let Ashura know that I'm leaving and get my bag or whatever. Give me like one minute."

29

Ashura ran her sweaty palms down her jeans as she looked over at Anthony, who was deep on his phone.

“Bae, are you nervous?” Ashura’s brows drew together when he didn’t respond to her. “Anthony?!”

Anthony’s head snapped up, with a smile he spoke, “What is it, baby girl?”

“Are you nervous?” She restated with a nervous facial expression.

Anthony was on cloud nine; he wasn’t nervous at all. In fact, he was the opposite of that. He was on another level happy. “Not at all. I’m just waiting to see how far along you are. I think you may have gotten pregnant before Fiji. If that’s the case, then that means you would be around three months. That means we ain't got a lot of time to get her room and shit together…”

“How do you know it’s a girl?”

Anthony smiled. “I got a feeling. If she come out looking like you, I already know I’m gon’ have to pop me a nigga or two for wanting to fuck with my shawty.”

Ashura smiled at the seriousness of his expression. At that moment, the doctor walked into the room. Ashura immediately recognized him as the doctor that attended to Cole when he was taken through emergency when he was shot.

“Wait… what kind of doctor are you?”

The doctor smiled at her before he set her chart down. “Let’s just say, I’m a jack of all trades.”

Ashura looked at Anthony for answers, but he just smiled. “This is my frat brother… Raheem, also known as freak nasty Stone.”

Raheem shook his head. “Can you be professional for once?”

“Stone?” Ashura stated with a frown on her face. “Stone the doctor? Really?”

Raheem chuckled as he reached his hand out to Ashura, waiting for her to shake it. Ashura eased her hand into his, suspicion in her eyes.

“Raheem, this is my future wife, Ashura.”

“Nice to meet you,” Stone stated, dropping a smile on Ashura.

“Uh- huh,” Ashura replied.

"Raheem, Cole, and I go way back. We went to college together, but Stone changed schools' freshman year. We just linked back up with his ass a few weeks ago. "

"Yeah," Ashura mumbled absently, still trying to put two and two together.

"So, I understand you have a bun…"

"You were a part of that experiment too, weren't you?"

Raheem dropped his head, and Anthony chuckled. "I swear, my baby don't miss shit."

"That's why you helped Cole. That's why I'm here. Is this some sort of inner circle?"

Raheem smiled. "You can think of it like that. It's a little unorthodox."

"It's a lot unorthodox. Where is your certification?"

Raheem smiled as he went to his wallet to grab his wallet size diploma.

Ashura took it and examined it closely. "Let me see your id!"

Raheem looked at Anthony who just shrugged. "Seriously?"

"Bae wanna see that shit, let bae see that shit."

30

He heard her.

Drawn to her, he left his office to tend to the sound coming from her room.

He stood in the doorway of his guestroom and listened to his name being whispered from Nacobi's lips. It caused his entire body to react. The fine hair all over his body stood on end when she moaned deep within her throat.

He licked his lips as she rolled over on her back and ran her hand down the front of her body, her manicured fingers settling between her legs, lifting the thin fabric of her teddy as she ran her hands all the way up to her breast. He didn't know if she was sleep or not, he couldn't tell from this distance, but he knew she was either fantasizing about him or dreaming. Either way, she was craving him the way he was craving her and that was all the motivation he needed to put both of them out of their misery.

Removing his muscle shirt as he walked over to her, left in only his gray sweat pants that she told him he was only allowed to wear while they were inside- hanging off his hips in a manner that left most of his torso exposed, he stood at the edge of the bed.

She must have fallen asleep with the music on, because now that he was closer, he could hear the soft sound of Eric Bellinger, playing from the Beats pill that sat on the nightstand next to the bed she laid in.

Nacobi released a curse as the air in the room seemed to heat at a temperature that was extremely uncomfortable. Her eyes peeled open slowly, taking in the figure that stood above her.

She wasn't scared. Not by a long shot. If anything, his presence confirmed her suspicions that he was close. She did need him. After fighting the urge to have him for so long, she was done with that shit.

"You called me, Nano?"

Nacobi tucked her bottom lip into her mouth and nodded her head before she released her lip and inhaled. "I don't want to want you."

"Too bad, sweetheart," Cole crooned as he reached for Nacobi's foot. Stepping forward, he placed a kiss on her ankles, letting his tongue touch her flesh before he moved his kisses up to her lower leg, all the while looking into her eyes. He dwelled at the moment, closing his eyes to inhale the feminine scent of her, missing it to the point where he pondered coming into her room or showing up at her house, just to have her more than likely reject him. But now that he had her with him, where he wanted her to be, at the edge of his fingertips, with her confessing to him that she wanted him, he was more than ready to oblige her.

He kissed the front of her thigh, before moving to the inside of her thigh, trailing kisses up her body as his hand pressed into the bed as he crawled over her.

“Give me your tongue.”

It wasn’t a request, so Nacobi quickly maneuvered her tongue out of her mouth. The moment Cole saw it, his mouth watered. Taking his tongue, he ran his over hers before he greedily kissed her.

Nacobi felt her brain go mush as she wrapped her arms around Cole’s neck to keep him in place, not wanting the kiss between them to end. She moved her hands to run them down his chest as he continued to kiss her. Slow. Almost to the point of dizziness, she felt him shifting to remove her teddy. She moved up so that he could take it off and spread her legs so that he could settle between them before he reached up to grab her breast.

Cole took his time, catering to every area of her body. Everything that he missed. The parts of her that he yearned. Places on her that he memorized; like the birthmark right below her breast and the beauty mark that rested right beneath her bellybutton.

Nacobi's entire body shivered when Cole lifted her thighs, parting them to place his face at the core of her. "Cole…"

Cole licked his lips, his stomach growling though he was full, he still craved her. He used his finger to part her lips before sending his tongue over her, groaning as her taste coaxed his tongue.

He slid his tongue back into his mouth and savored it. "Damn, Nano," he exclaimed as he returned to the task of tasting her.

Nacobi moaned before she placed her hand on his shoulders, then moved to his head as she seemingly guided his mouth to the places that needed his attention the most, as if he needed direction.

She felt him slither two fingers into her before his tongue flicked over her clit, before he kissed it, pulled it between his lips and slurped on her until she was cummin in his mouth. It happened quick, so quick that it took Nacobi off guard. She tried to grab Cole, but he grabbed her arm, preventing her from moving.

"Fuccckkkk," she groaned out as her entire body succumbed to Cole. Her thighs clenched around his head as her body continued to yield to his tongue. Taking her off her square and far beyond anything she could control. Her stomach clenched with each flick of his tongue, her toes curled, and her heart slammed into her chest.

Her eyes rolled to the back of her head as he finally released her and moved to remove his sweats. Through hooded eyes, she could see her juices glistening in his beard as he stuck his tongue out to lick the remnants of her off his lips.

Cole was content. As content as he'd been in a long time. Hearing his name fall off of Nacobi's lips in the heat of passion was enough for him, but he knew she needed more.

He reached for his dick, stroking it a few times before he moved up the bed. Grabbing Nacobi and kissing her lips again before he began to feed her, placing the head of his manhood at her entrance while licking his lips. He looked drunk as if he'd been drinking all night when in fact he hadn't drunk anything at all.

Cole looked into Nacobi's eyes, feeling her heat take him in. She released a low moan.

"I fucking miss you, Nano."

Nacobi knew he wasn't speaking to her directly, but more so to the part of her that made her a woman. She knew he missed her as well, but right now, he was talking to her pussy. She didn't feel a way at all, in fact, she missed his dick possibly just as much as he missed her pussy.

Nacobi placed her hand on Cole's chest, but he slapped it away before grabbing her wrist and placing her arm above her head.

"What you want, Nano? Speak now or forever hold that shit."

Nacobi went to tell him that it didn't matter how he made love to her, as long as he did it. But before she could respond to him, he began to feed her more of him.

Never the one to back down, Nacobi pulled her legs up and rested them against his side so that he could gain more access to her.

Cole took that opportunity to get deeper inside of her. Their eyes stayed connected until Cole was as so deep inside of Nacobi that her legs shook.

Cole looked down as he pulled back, watching his dick come out of her covered in her juices. He smirked, "Nano, type shit," he mumbled as his body flexed, fighting the pull she had over him.

Cole leaned down to kiss Nacobi as the wetness of Nano seemingly drowned him. Nacobi released small moans that made goosebumps form all over his skin.

He lifted her legs and pumped into her slowly, his eyes never leaving hers as she moaned his name over and over, a melody he loved and missed.

Nacobi's eyes fluttered closed as she fought to keep them open.

31

Cole stood in the shadows, twisting his neck from left to right, waiting.

He continued to wait…not seeing any signs of his target. This job was overdue. Way overdue. There wasn't anything that would prevent this from happening. His soul needed it.

Once he walked out of the bar, stumbling and talking on the phone to someone, Cole eased onto his bike.

"Man… fuck that nigga! I want you back, Nacobi!"

Cole slid the helmet of his mask down before looking over his shoulder at Romeo. He didn't understand why he was on the phone with Nacobi. She wasn't his lifeline… she was Cole's. Plus, it was too damn late to phone a friend.

"Ayeeee! You gone let me come through and fuck? I know that nigga ain't hitting it right! Hello?! Hello?!"

Romeo grunted as he slid his phone into his pocket. "This some bullshit!"

He grabbed his keys out of his pocket, fumbling with them before he was able to get the door unlocked the door. “I'm getting my Nano back! Fuck that nigga!”

That statement, *My Nano*, fucked with Cole’s system. He closed his eyes, placing his feet on the ground on each side of his bike, he checked his gun to make sure the safety was off. Once Romeo was comfortable in his car, turning the key to start the engine, Cole eased onto his gas.

He hit a u- turn in the middle of the street, burning rubber, making a huge cloud of smoke. Oohs and aahs came from the intoxicated audience that had formed outside of the bar.

Cole created a large enough cloud to cover his mission before he eased his bike up beside Romeo’s car. He used the barrel of the gun to tap on the partially open window.

Romeo looked up in time to see the gun pointed at his head.

“You don’t listen. I told you to stay away. My Fucking Nano!”

Cole emptied the gun in Romeo, leaving the last bullet in the chamber for a headshot before he zoomed off, out of the cloud of smoke.

His next stop, Danielle’s. Initially, he didn’t want to kill Danielle but she presented a threat to his life and the life of the woman that he loved. He couldn’t allow her to continue in her attempts to find Vince. Yes, he knew of that and he wanted to get ahead of it before it became a bigger problem.

After learning that Danielle was physically abusive to her son, Cole knew the child would be better off with his father.

He rode his bike to her address, knocked on her door and shot her point-blank range before leaving out and returning home.

Cole stood on his patio, coffee in hand, looking out at the lake that was the selling point of the property. He needed the serenity, and the lake was always the thing that provided it, well that, and the woman that was still asleep in his bed.

Nacobi heard him when he entered the door, she had been up waiting for him to return.

Cole went to speak but she stopped him.

"You were right about me," She spoke in a low broken voice. "All the things you said about me not knowing how to handle a man like you. You were right and a part of me hated the fact that you were right, Cole. I hated it because I wanted to be the one to control how I reacted to you. How you made me feel and when I thought I lost you, I hated you more for the pain I caused myself. I should have never questioned you. I should have trusted you to be there for me like you always have been.

Thank you, Cole. For… everything that you've ever done for me. I love you. I want you to always know that. I don't know what the future holds for us. I don't know if we will ever be able to get this right, but I want you to know that I love you. When my dad told me everything, what you are to me, I didn't want to believe it. But something about you has always stuck with me. You caught me off guard, and I'm defenseless against you. My heart is yours, Cole, and I'm sorry if I pushed you away. I just… I didn't know what pure love looked like. I didn't know how to accept it. I'm so used to bullshit but if you would forgive me and give me a chance to love you right, I promise to never take advantage of it again. Please?"

Cole stood there, taking in the beauty that spoke to him and wondered if she were capable of love on the level that she was offering. He was fucked up… but so was she in a lot of ways.

Epilogue

Ashura smiled at Nacobi as she walked toward her. She was beautiful, glowing, happy. She almost looked angelic.

“Don’t smile at me, bitch,” Nacobi snapped.

Ashura’s smile dropped. “…and then there’s that.”

“This is stupid.”

Ashura frowned at her friend as she adjusted her daughter in her arms. “What do you mean it’s stupid? It's your baby shower.”

“I don’t want to have all these folk in my house, man. Wanting to rub my stomach and shit. It's annoying.”

Ashura rolled her eyes. “Something is seriously wrong with you.”

Nacobi scrunched up her face. “Well…”

Ashura chuckled as she bounced Zaire in her lap. “I really have a hard time dealing with you.”

“Stop bouncing her,” Nacobi snapped. “She doesn’t like that shit!”

"How would you know what she likes?"

"Because I know, just stop."

Ashura stopped bouncing Zaire, which caused her baby to look up at her as if she was crazy. Ashura leaned down and kissed Zaire, who broke out in giggles.

Anthony walked into the room where his wife and daughter sat, watching them made a grin split his face. He couldn't recall a time when he had been this happy. Never. Never had he been this happy. He has everything he wanted in life, all before he hit the age of thirty. Some people spend their lifetimes looking for the joy he had. He was not a fool. He counted his blessings. Counted them two and three times, and thanked GOD for everything that he ever received.

Ashura looked up when she saw him enter the room. Zaire, who was a splitting image of Ashura, reached her chubby arms up the minute she saw her daddy. Anthony smiled as he bent down to grab her, placing a kiss on her cheek and making her laugh.

"You want your daddy," Anthony asked as he tickled Zaire, who would be a year-old next month.

Anthony loved everything about fatherhood. From Zaire's personality to her goofy moments in learning to walk. The late nights. The early mornings. Everything.

"I'm dealing with grumpy over here," Ashura said to Anthony as he sat beside her.

Anthony looked at Nacobi. “What you fussin’ about now?”

Nacobi crossed her arms over her chest and shrugged. “I don’t want to do this,” she spoke in a low voice. “I don’t know why Ashura insists.”

“It's what normal people do, Nacobi.”

“I ain't normal, though,” Nacobi said, sticking her hand out in confusion. “The fuck?”

“Stop being mean.”

Nacobi looked at the door and rolled her eyes again.

Cole walked into the room, grinning at her.

“I ain't even trying to hear what the fuck you talking about.”

Cole wrapped his arms around Nacobi, causing her to blush. Cole kissed the side of her face before leaning forward to look into her eyes. “Stop giving everyone a hard time.”

“Cole,” Nacobi snapped. “This is extra.”

The *this* she was referring to was the matching custom attire Ashura insisted that they wear, matching the theme of the baby shower, and the over the top gender reveal that is scheduled for later on in the evening.

Cole smiled. “She’s just excited, sweetheart. Don’t give her a hard time.”

“Thank you!” Ashura exclaimed as she looked at her best friend. Ashura was in awe of the progress that Nacobi and Cole had made, they went from literally not being able to get it right, to loving each other so deep that it bordered on being weird. Cole knew how to keep Nacobi in line, and Nacobi knew how to keep Cole centered. They were made for each other.

“She’s extra,” Nacobi spat.

“Are you excited to find out what we are having?” Cole asked.

“I could have been known if this wanch hadn’t stolen my sonogram from the doctor before I could see it. Threatened Stone with bodily harm if he told me what I was having.”

“Damn right,” Ashura added.

“Let's just go and get this over with. My feet hurt, and I'm hungry.”

Cole smiled in admiration of Nacobi. He was a happy man. He couldn’t ask GOD for much else. It would just be too much for him to handle.

The End!

Crowned 2: The Return of a Savage

If you would like to attend the rest of the baby shower and find out the gender of Nacobi and Cole's baby...

#JoinDreamzTeam

& attend the Book Discussion for an extended version of the baby shower scene!

DreamzTeam Reader's Lounge

Thank you so much for reading!! I love y'all!

www.liveindreamz.com for paperbacks and merchandise.

@Deshon Dreamz on Social Media!

CPSIA information can be obtained
at www.ICGtesting.com
Printed in the USA
LVOW13s2255240817
546235LV00016BA/2079/P